AN ORPHAN'S ESCAPE

HISTORICAL VICTORIAN SAGA

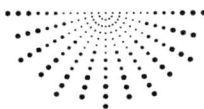

ROSIE SWAN

PUREREAD.COM

CONTENTS

1. Destiny Can't Be Stopped — 1
2. More Than Dreams — 14
3. Hoping for Better — 24
4. Prayers in the Night — 33
5. Lamentations for Love — 48
6. The Undesirable Elements — 58
7. Whoever Loves, Believes — 70
8. Night of Terror — 85
9. Damsel in Distress — 95
10. Broken Promises — 105
11. A Long Way from Home — 118
12. Worlds Apart — 130
13. The Tide Will Turn — 142
14. The Day the Rain Came Down — 153
15. Darkness Has Passed — 167
16. The Morning Comes — 178
17. The Evils That Men Do — 188
18. Deep Considerations — 194
19. Time of Grace — 201
20. New Beginnings — 210
    Epilogue — 216

Love Victorian Romance? — 221
Our Gift To You — 223

1
DESTINY CAN'T BE STOPPED

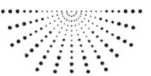

846 – Ritter's Village, Cambridge, North East England

Malone Manor! It was hard for six-year-old Constance Baker to believe that this was their new home. Less than a month ago her family had been unaware of the existence of this estate let alone this magnificent house. And the estate was large. Her eyes had grown larger and rounder as the fancy carriage that brought them here rolled through acres and acres of rich and fertile land. She'd seen horses out in the meadow and too many cows to count and her small ears had perked when she heard her parents talking about the new life they were going to lead from that moment.

They had moved from their small, three-room cottage in Alperton, Ipswich, where they sometimes went without food. It had been quite crowded for the family of seven and their neighbours were as poor as they were, with most of the menfolk working at the small flour mill just like her father. But Connie had loved it in Alperton because she'd had many friends there, children like her who dressed in old and tattered clothes. She had enjoyed running around the small field behind their house and also, her parents had been too busy trying to eke out a living to pay much attention to her and her four siblings. As the eldest child she had had to look after her siblings when her parents were working away from home, but she still found some time to play with her friends. Unlike here where all she did was work while her siblings played.

Connie sighed as her eyes roamed around the backyard. She could hear chickens clucking while pigs snorted and cows mooed in the distance. It was a very large estate and there were four barns plus the large stable. She loved sneaking into the stable to look at the horses, and she felt that they understood her whenever she whispered to them. Her favourite horse was a black mare that had white patches all over its body. She'd found out from one of the stablemen that this particular horse was called Polka Dot. Whenever the six-year-old could, she would slip into Polka Dot's stall and talk to her, just like she'd done today. She really wished someone would teach her how to ride. Maybe she would ask her mother to allow her to get some riding lessons when her siblings were being taught.

But she now had to go back to the house, or manor, as her mother insisted on all the children calling their home. It was so many times larger than their cottage home in Alperton. Now they lived in splendour, and there was so much luxury around them that it was like a dream. Well, it was a dream for her family, but for Connie nothing had really changed. She missed her friends back in Ipswich and knew that she would never see them again.

From the moment her parents had arrived home one day and announced that they were moving, things had changed. For one, Connie and her siblings had been forbidden from talking to the neighbours.

"Our lot in life has changed and these people are just jealous of us,"ial her mother had cried out. "We don't belong here anymore and will never return to this forsaken village."

The one thing that made Connie miss their old life even more was the fact that these days her parents were always at home. Being rich and living in this fancy house meant that they no longer went out to work, and that made them take too much notice of the children. Connie hated it because now her parents found any and every reason to shout at her or strike her. How she missed their old life, but that was something she would never say out loud, ever again. The first and only time she'd expressed a desire to return to Ipswich, she'd received a resounding slap from her mother.

"You are a good-for-nothing girl," Mrs. Dinah Baker had screamed at her terrified six-year-old daughter, her oldest child. "We came from a life of poverty and are now living like kings and queens, and yet you want us to go back to that horrible life we lived before. What kind of a child are you?"

Connie had held her cheek and let the tears fall, and even now as she recalled the hard slap, she winced, remembering the pain. Her small hand went up to her cheek and she felt the tears. Hearing pattering feet coming her way, she quickly wiped her eyes and pretended to smile. It was her two sisters and they sped past her toward the kitchen door.

"Come and see my bedroom," her sister Mary who was five years old called out to Anne, who was four. "Mama put fresh flowers in my room," the two girls held hands and walked past Connie without saying a single word to her, their little noses in the air.

It had always been like this; her two sisters doing things together and leaving her out. That was the reason she had loved living in Ipswich because the neighbours' children had been her friends. From when she had begun to reason, she'd noticed that her parents treated her differently. But out in Ipswich it hadn't been so obvious because of their neighbours, who looked out for each other. No child could cry without the neighbours asking if the little one was ill or hungry. And the neighbours frowned upon any parents who caned their children without good reason.

While they lived in the small cottage in Ipswich, her four siblings had shared one bedroom while their parents had the second one. Connie had to sleep on the hearth in the living room.

During summer it was comfortable enough because the small cottage got very hot. But in winter it would get very cold, and sometimes her parents would light a fire in the living room but most times they went to bed and left her sleeping on the cold floor with just an old shawl to cover herself with.

But then her parents had come home a month ago looking very excited, and Connie heard them telling her siblings that they were moving to a big house. They had talked about the stables with many horses, the barn with cows and the sty with pigs, as well as chickens in the coop. And then they had moved here, and Connie thought they were living in a castle. The manor was so big that she got lost in the house a few times before finally learning to make her way around.

She had stared in wonder at the large manor and when her mother allocated rooms, the little girl expected that she would have one of the pretty rooms. There were seven bedrooms in the house, three downstairs and four on the first floor. These were all fully furnished with very comfortable beds.

Being the curious child that she was, Connie had gone into one of the bedrooms on the first floor when she saw her siblings doing the same and climbed on the comfortable bed. Sighing with relief she started dozing off until the door was opened roughly.

"What are you doing here?" her mother rushed into the bedroom. "You're a worthless child," and proceeded to give her a thorough beating. "Your kind cannot sleep in a bed," and grabbed her by the ear, dragging her up the narrow stairs at the end of the corridor to the attic. She pushed her into the dark room. "This is your room and if I ever find you in one of the other bedchambers, you'll be sorry that you were ever born."

That was a month ago and life had only seemed to get worse in the days since. Connie sighed as she entered the kitchen, the one place where she had a little peace from her siblings and parents.

"What were you doing outside?" Mrs. Eve, the elderly cook, frowned at Connie when she entered the warm kitchen, shivering like she'd been standing in the rain. "It's really cold and you don't have any warm clothing. You'll catch cold and get sick. Come and sit here beside the fire. Don't you have any cardigans?" Connie shook her head, moving closer to the fire and sinking down gratefully. "Here, have this cup of hot chocolate, but you better take it quickly before your Mama comes in here and begins to yell at you."

"Thank you," Connie said, moving to the corner and sipping the warm chocolate. Mrs. Eve also brought her a thick cookie and she ate it hurriedly.

The next day Mrs. Eve brought some old clothes for Connie. "These belonged to my granddaughter, but she has outgrown them. Make sure that you keep them hidden from your Mama or she will even burn them."

"Yes Ma'am."

Christmas Day that year was snowy, and the family gathered in the living room where Mr. Baker had lit a merry fire.

Connie kept wiping her tears because her parents hadn't bought her any presents. Come to think of it, she'd never received any presents during Christmas, but it hadn't hurt as much before. Even young as she was, she'd understood that there wasn't any money for presents. And back in Alperton, she and her friends had learned how to make small toys from the rags they collected from Mr. Simon, the tailor. They had made little dolls and played with them but all the toys she'd collected over the years had been tossed out by her mother when they moved to Malone Manor.

But now they were wealthy, and she had seen the numerous packages her parents had carried into the house. Excited that she would finally get a new dress and shoes, Connie had waited to receive her own, but finally realized that it wasn't going to happen.

Standing forlornly at the door leading to the hallway, she watched as her siblings unwrapped their presents while dressed in new clothes and shoes.

"Mama," Connie took a step further into the living room. But she was careful to stand closer to the door.

"What do you want?" Her father snarled at her and she shrank against the door.

"Is there a present for me?" Though she was scared of the ugly look on her father's face, her young eyes blazed with hope. Maybe they had forgotten to give her the presents they had bought for her because they were very busy.

"You want a present?"

She wiped her eyes and nodded, an expectant smile on her face.

"The only present suitable for a worthless girl like you is to tidy the mess the other children leave behind," her father said. "Now get up and leave my presence before I trample you to dust."

Young as she was, that was the last time that Connie ever asked her parents for any presents or anything else. She never wanted to humiliated like that again, and she slunk out of the living room.

"What happened to you?" Mrs. Eve looked at the small girl whose face bore tear stains, her lips tightened.

"Nothing," Connie wiped her tears, but more took their place. She wanted to sob out loudly but knew that if her father heard her, he would probably come and reprimand her.

"Come," Mrs. Eve took her hand and led her to her usual spot in front of the hearth. "Sit down and don't make a sound at all, do you hear me?"

"Yes."

When Connie went to bed that night, she was actually smiling. Even though her family had ignored her the whole day, Mrs. Eve had made it the best Christmas Day for her. From feeding her sweet pies to telling her the story of the first Christmas, Connie felt that she had the best day of them all. And Mrs. Eve had even brought her a ragdoll which had belonged to her granddaughter. It was old but still very pretty and Connie fell in love with it as soon as it was handed to her. Mrs. Eve charged her to keep it hidden at all times and only play with it when she was alone.

Yes, Mrs. Eve had told her of the Little Baby Boy who was born in Bethlehem long ago and who was the Saviour of the world.

"Never forget that Jesus loves you, dear child, even if others do not. And His love is forever," Mrs. Eve had told her and as she fell asleep, her pretty ragdoll in her arms, she thought about the Little Baby Boy in Bethlehem who loved her.

"Mrs. Baker, you were here a few days ago and I gave you enough money to cover your expenses for the month," Mr. Edgar Blackwell stared at the woman seated in her office. "I also gave you a tidy sum as a Christmas bonus even though you didn't deserve it since you're not a servant. Only servants receive Christmas bonuses, but I made an exception in your case. Don't make me regret doing that."

Mrs. Dinah Baker clutched her purse close to her chest, feeling very angry at the way the solicitor was treating her.

"Mr. Blackwell, you know that children go through clothes and outgrow their shoes very fast. It's the New Year and I need to get new things for them. You have children and understand what I'm talking about."

Mr. Blackwell shook his head, "I'm sorry, but the terms of Mr. David Malone's will were very clear. You are to get a specific amount of money each month for expenses and nothing more. This amount goes up by ten percent every year but there's no way that it can be increased each month just to suit your finer tastes," he said this sardonically, but the irate woman chose to ignore his tone.

"But how am I supposed to take care of the house expenses when the money isn't enough?"

Mr. Blackwell fixed his eyes on her, his grey eyes very cold and hard. "The amount you're getting is enough for your monthly needs. Come back for more next month. What's more, you're living freely on Mr. Malone's estate and everything has been provided for you. The servants' wages are paid directly from Mr. David's estate for as long as they work there. The only expenses you have to worry about are those concerned with buying food. You have plenty of cows and chickens that feed you and your family. What more do you want? And yet you got your usual stipend as usual? And that amount that has been allocated to you is quite sufficient. As for the clothes, that is what the Christmas bonus was to be used for. I really don't understand how you could have gone through so much money in such a short time. Are you building another manor?" His eyebrows were raised, and she felt slighted. These rich people looked down on those who weren't well off as themselves! Her lips tightened, she deserved to be treated with respect now that her lot in life had changed. No longer would she remain silent as some rich solicitor tried to make her feel worthless.

"I will find another solicitor and overturn that will," Mrs. Baker hissed as she rose to her feet. "The money you're giving me is not enough and I demand more."

But Mr. Blackwell was done with the contentious woman and also rose to his feet. "I have other important and urgent obligations to attend to, so if you will please excuse me," he pointed at the door.

Mrs. Baker slammed the door hard on her way out and Mr. Blackwell winced. But he wasn't about to give in to the troublesome woman. He couldn't believe that it had only been about six months since she had taken control of Malone Estate. Yet the woman now behaved like a real born-into-wealth socialite, a very greedy one at that. He shook his head, glad to be rid of her. Had it been up to him, he wouldn't have let the likes of Mrs. Dinah Baker anywhere near the estate, but he was only carrying out the instructions he'd been given by Mr. David Malone.

Mrs. Dinah Baker was fuming because she needed money to settle some very unpleasant debts. The worst was the one she owed to Henry Pitcher, her husband's very good friend.

"This is all because of your own stupidity," she muttered to herself. Their indiscretions had started four years ago and had led to Henry blackmailing her when he realised that she wasn't going to leave her husband for him. Now the imbecile was threatening to tell Gerald about their relationship.

Gerald was a very vile-tempered man and if he as much as suspected her of having had an illicit relationship with his friend there was no telling what he would do. Henry was waiting for money from her and she just had to convince him to be patient.

"Did you bring the money?" Were the first words Henry Pitcher uttered to Dinah as she stepped into his living room. He was sprawled out on the couch looking very much at ease. Though he was over forty years old, he still looked very attractive, and Dinah rued the day she had set her eyes on him. He was a very charming man and had easily seduced her, promising her the world, the sun and the stars as well, and she had stupidly believed him. Were it not for Mr. Malone leaving her the estate, she had already decided to leave her husband for him. But now that she was no longer dependant on him for financial assistance, the man was doing all he could to hurt her. There was a half-filled bottle of whisky and a full glass on the coffee table in front of him. "I told you that I'm running out of all patience with you."

"Mr. Blackwell said he will get me some money next week. Please be patient," Dinah Baker begged for all she was worth. "I promise that I will bring you a substantial amount when I come next week."

He scratched his chin, his eyes leery and full of wickedness, and she shuddered inwardly. She knew that look and it was what had got her into trouble many times before. "If you don't have my money, then you know what you have to do."

"Please Henry, not today. I have to go home because I told Gerald that I wouldn't stay out late."

"If you don't want me to tell Gerald about what has been happening the last four years, then I suggest that you go up to my bedroom and wait there for me."

"You have as much to lose as I do if you tell my husband, and I have a mind to confess to him," Dinah threatened, hoping to intimidate her lover who was also her nemesis. But Henry just threw his head back and laughed at her.

"You really think you can stand up to me, Dinah Baker? I suggest you think again before making such foolish threats to me. You can continue living your pretend life of being a respectable wife and mother, but one word from me and it will all come tumbling down" his sardonic smile irked her.

Just then a knock at the door interrupted their conversation. Henry stood to open the door, and outside stood a grubby little man or questionable heritage. Dinah supposed this was one of Henry's questionable business associates.

"Get out of here, woman," he growled. Dinah was relieved to obey, scurrying toward the open door, but Henry's hand grabbed her. Pulling her to himself he whispered something in her ear before releasing her. She was spared, this time, but the heavy threat of exposure hung heavy over her head.

It was getting dark and she knew that her husband would be waiting for her. She just hoped that he would be in a mellow mood.

"One day I will do something to get rid of him," she swore under her breath as she hurried down his driveway taking care not to be seen by his servants. Henry Pitcher was becoming too dangerous and demanding and she didn't want anything or anyone to interfere with the plans she had for her future life.

In the past, when they had lived in Alperton in near poverty, Henry, who was part owner of the flour mill where Gerald worked, had provided for her, and that was what led to their illicit relationship. He claimed to be in love with her and had ranted and raved when she told him she wouldn't leave her husband for him. Now that she lived in the manor, her one desire was to be considered as a respectable and wealthy woman and accepted by her high-society neighbours. This is what had been her lifelong dream and the last thing she wanted was for anyone to find out what was going on between her and Henry Pitcher. Gerald and Mr. Blackwell could never find out what was going on.

Henry Pitcher could cost her dearly, and now that she'd tasted of the good life, she didn't want it to end. The man's parting words a few minutes ago frightened her.

"Mr. Blackwell is a puritan and if he ever suspects you of any indiscretions, you will lose everything," his eyes were full of malice. "So I suggest that you keep me happy, or the said gentleman will have a little bird whispering something in his ears."

Just as she'd feared, Gerald was waiting for her. "Where have you been all this time?" He asked as soon as she entered their bedroom. She hadn't seen him and gave a yelp of surprise.

"And why do you look so skittish like those mares in the stable?"

"It's nothing," she said hurriedly, turning away to take off her jewellery. "I went to see Amanda Kenton because she asked me to help her with her high tea sometime next week. Her son is returning from Europe and she wants it to be a fanciful affair," she knew she was blabbering but couldn't stop herself. At least she had passed by Amanda's house earlier in the day and knew that the lady would cover for her should Gerald go there to ask. After all, even Amanda had her own indiscretions and Dinah often covered for her with her husband.

"Are we invited to that high tea?" Dinah nearly sagged with relief when her husband lost his suspicious look. "Mr. Kenton is a well-known fellow and I'd like him to introduce me to the high society around here. After all, we have to live and look the part of wealthy landowners."

"Of course," Dinah laughed and linked her hand in his. "Mrs. Kenton said she would give me our invitation when I go there tomorrow to finish up with the preparations."

"You are a good woman," Gerald said. "We need to do all we can so we can be a part of this community and be respected. You and I, my dear wife, are going places."

2
MORE THAN DREAMS

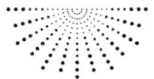

It was just four months after his mother's death that Abel Pierson's father, Joel, sat him down to inform him of the changes that were going to take place in their lives. The ten-year-old looked at his father with wide eyes and growing dismay as he spoke of someone else coming into their lives.

"Her name is Mrs. Anita Dawson and she is a widow with no children," Joel Pierson was saying. "I want you to welcome her and treat her as if she were your own mother."

"Pa, will Mrs. Dawson live here with us?"

"Of course, why do you ask?"

Abel looked around their two-room cottage, then back to his father. "Where will she sleep?"

"In my bedroom, of course," the thirty-year-old man smiled at his son. Every time he looked at Abel he saw his beloved wife in his son's face. Abel had Caroline's green eyes and sandy brown hair. He missed his wife, but life had to go on, and his son needed a mother. "I know that we moved your cot to my bedroom these past few months after your Mama died, but now you have to return to sleeping in the living room."

"Why?"

"Because Mrs. Dawson and I will now sleep in the same bedroom since we are getting married."

"But that's where Mama used to sleep. Mrs. Dawson can't sleep in Ma's bed," Abel said forcefully.

"Your mother is dead," Joel tried to be as patient as he could while explaining to his son about how people moved on with their lives when loved ones died. "Mrs. Dawson will be your new mother and I want you to love and respect her."

"I'll try, Pa."

But much as Abel tried to love his new stepmother, she didn't mellow toward him. And she even told him never to call her 'Mother,' but only when his father wasn't present. Mrs. Dawson wasn't as pretty as his Mama had been and he felt angry when she wore his mother's dresses and shoes. But his father was happy and that was what mattered. Ma had made him promise that he would always make Pa happy. He kept his mouth shut but smouldered inside.

With his mother gone there was no way he was going to stay around the cottage with Mrs. Dawson who clearly didn't want him there. So he started following his father to the Manor to work with the horses. Mr. David Malone had let him play around the stable, but with the new family that had moved in recently, his father didn't want any trouble and so discouraged the boy from following him.

Abel loved horses; he actually loved all animals that were on the estate and was good friends with those who took care of them. Randy Dickson and Nicholas Green liked sending him on errands and they would give him coins, which he stored in a small bottle that was hidden in the ground in their woodshed at the cottage. He was saving to buy himself a horse one day and then he would never stop riding. Maybe he would even ride to lands far away and see the world.

"What are you doing hiding down here?" Joel found his son in one of the stalls. "You should be at home with your mother."

"But Pa, she says that I am getting under her feet and should stay away. Please, can I stay here with you and the horses?"

"Don't be an insolent child. Now go home at once and be obedient to your mother. Or else I'll take a whip to your hide."

Abel scrunched his face in annoyance and stomped out of the stable. Why couldn't his father understand that he loved being near horses more than with his stepmother? Well, he was going but he wouldn't be ending up at home. Instead he would go hunting, and his small face brightened at the idea.

But just as he was about to set foot on the path that led to the woods, he heard someone crying. He nearly dismissed the sound as that of one of the wild cats that roamed the woods at night, but something urged him to go and check. The sniffling sounds were coming from behind the manor's large woodshed and he went to check.

He found a small girl staring at a pile of wood, tears coursing down her face. She was really pretty even though her face was flushed, and her eyes were red because of so much crying.

"Did someone hurt you?" He approached slowly so as not to alarm her. He'd seen her many times at the manor and wondered who she was because she never played with the other four snobbish children. "Why are you crying?"

"I don't know how to chop wood," Connie wiped her nose with the back of her hand. "But Mama wants me to chop all this wood before dinner time."

Abel frowned, looking at the pile of wood and then at the little girl and finally at the large axe he knew she couldn't even lift, let alone use to chop wood.

"Why would your mother tell you to chop all this wood and you're so little? Can you even lift that axe?"

"Because there's no wood in the house," Connie gave an impatient look. "Who are you?"

"My name is Abel Pierson and I live in one of the cottages in the wood. My father takes care of Mr. Malone's horses. What's your name?" Her hair was golden and her eyes so blue that he thought he was looking at the sky. She was really pretty.

"Constance, but people call me Connie," she looked around and tried to pick up the axe which was lying at her feet. It was too heavy, and she dropped it, nearly crushing her foot with it.

"Be careful," Abel cried out. "You could hurt yourself."

"What will I do?" Connie started crying again.

"Connie, don't cry. Let me run home and bring the axe my Pa had the blacksmith forge for me. It's lighter and then I will help you chop this wood. Stop crying now."

And Connie nodded, wiping her face. "See," she gave him such a beautiful smile that even though he was ten years old, he made up his mind right then that this girl was special, and that their meeting today was not an accident. He found himself responding to her smile. "I'm not crying again."

"Good," he nodded. "Now wait here and don't try to lift that big axe again. I don't want you hurting yourself."

"I will wait for you," and saying so, she sat on a small stump, all tears forgotten.

Abel rushed home and avoiding the house, made his way to the small shed at the back of their house. He'd helped his father build this woodshed while his mother was still alive. Spotting the axe, he picked it up and started back to the manor.

"Abel, come here at once," he heard his stepmother's shrill voice but chose to ignore her summons. She must have seen him through the small window at the back of the house. He was sure that all she wanted was to cause trouble, but he didn't want to be delayed from his very important mission of putting a smile on Connie's face. "Abel!"

The little boy ran faster even though he knew that he would face his father later. His stepmother was sure to report to him that he had ignored her, and his father would definitely give him a beating. But that didn't matter because he was going to put a smile on the face of his new little friend.

"Here I am," he announced needlessly. "I'll chop the wood and you can arrange the pieces and then I'll help you carry them to the manor."

"No," Connie shook her head. "If Mama sees you, she will get very angry with me. I'll carry the wood by myself, you just go ahead and chop it."

"Very well then," he rolled up his sleeves the way he'd seen his father do so many times when he was getting down to do some hard work. At least the wood was dry enough to be easily chopped and he split it into thin pieces. "Why don't your sisters and brothers help you with the work?"

"They have to be in the schoolroom with Miss Owen so she can teach them how to read and write."

"My Mama taught me how to read and write, and Papa helps me when he's not too tired," Abel said proudly. "If you want, I can teach you."

"That would marvellous."

Connie sat on the same small stump as before and watched Abel as he worked. Whenever he had chopped up enough bits she would get up, pick them up and then arrange them into neat little rows to make it easy for her to carry back to the manor.

"Will these be enough?" Abel pointed at the neat little piles. There were about ten of them.

"Maybe a little more," Connie said. "Abel, won't your mother be needing you right now?"

He shook his head. "My Mama is not at home."

"But when she gets back, won't she need you to help her?"

Connie saw him stiffen; then he turned to her. "My Mama died five months ago, and now there's a new mother at home. Her name is Mrs. Dawson and she is Pa's new wife."

"What is your new mama like?"

Abel shrugged, "She's nice, I think."

Connie narrowed her eyes at him. There was something he wasn't telling her, but as she opened her mouth to ask him another question, she heard her mother calling out from the manor.

"I have to go back to the house," she picked up one of the piles. "Please go now before Mama decides to come here and check. She won't be happy if she finds you here."

"Are you sure you'll be alright?"

"Yes, now go."

"Can I come and see you again tomorrow?" Abel held his breath, waiting for her answer.

"Yes, you can, and thank you for helping me. Now please hurry and leave."

Abel nodded, swung his axe onto his shoulder and walked away. Connie watched him disappearing into the woods and smiled. She had a new friend now and she practically skipped back to the house. It reminded her of the days when they lived in Ipswich.

"Where have you been, you insolent child?" Her mother glared at her, clearly annoyed for some reason. But then her mother rarely needed a reason to be angry.

"Mama, I was chopping the wood as you asked me and now I'm bringing it to the house," Connie said hurriedly as she placed the first pile on the floor in the corner. "Let me go and get some more."

"Come here," her mother picked up one of the longer pieces. "Is this what you call chopping wood to nice pieces?" And she brought it down hard on Connie's shoulder and the child screamed.

Mrs. Eve was in the pantry and ran back into the kitchen and was just in time to grab Mrs. Baker's hand before it came down again.

"What do you think you're doing?" She asked. "Do you want to kill this child?"

"Go back to doing whatever it is that you were doing," Mrs. Baker hissed.

"You don't tell me what to do, Mrs. Baker," Mrs. Eve hissed back. "Mind yourself or I will tell Mr. Blackwell what is going on here."

Mrs. Baker tossed the piece of wood back on the floor, spat at Connie and went back into the hallway.

Connie was crying as she rubbed her shoulder. She had to go and carry more wood.

"Come here child and let me see," Mrs. Eve said in a tender voice and the child approached her. This was the only person in the house who cared about her. Mrs. Eve made a sound of distress as she touched Connie's shoulder, pushing the sleeve aside and seeing the ugly welt. Connie winced and shrank back.

"I'm sorry it hurts so much," Mrs. Eve told her. "Let me put some ointment on it," and she reached for a small bottle she kept on the windowsill. "I keep this here for when I hurt myself with the knives and pots," she smiled. "I'm really sorry that you're hurt."

Once the ointment was applied and Connie pronounced that her shoulder felt better, Mrs. Eve nodded. "Come, let's go and bring back the other wood."

"Thank you," Connie said. She didn't hesitate to slip her small hand into Mrs. Eve's when she held her large one out. The going was slow because Mrs. Eve complained of her knees being stiff, but Connie knew that as long as she was with her, her mother wouldn't hit her.

Mrs. Eve looked at the piles of wood and then back at Connie. "Somehow I find it hard to believe that you chopped all this wood. And with that heavy axe," she raised her eyebrows.

"My friend helped me," Connie said. "But please don't tell Mama because she will be very angry."

"Your friend?"

"Yes, his name is Abel. He brought his little axe that his Pa made for him and then chopped the wood for me."

They soon carried all the chopped wood to the house and for the rest of the evening, Connie stayed close to Mrs. Eve. In the whole household the elderly woman was the only one who stood up to her mother and protected her. But Mrs. Eve was sickly and didn't always come to the house. On the days the elderly woman was absent Connie did her very best to stay hidden, as far away from her step mother as possible.

"Don't go troubling your Mama now, do you hear me?" Mrs. Eve told the child as she was helping her wash the dishes that night after dinner. "Be a good girl and your Mama won't get angry with you."

"Yes Ma'am," Connie said.

When the kitchen was clean, Mrs. Eve held her hand out. "Come; let me take you to your bedroom now."

"Thank you, Mrs. Eve," Connie was always afraid of going up to her attic bedroom alone because her mother never left any candles burning for her to see her way. The hallway was usually very dark and each time she walked to her bedroom she imagined someone might be waiting to pounce on her.

Mrs. Eve carried a small lantern and when they got to the small attic, Connie stared at her small bed in dismay.

"Did you wet your bed, Child?"

"No," Connie felt the tears well up in her eyes. Her blanket and mattress were soaked with water. The floor was also wet, and she knew that this was the work of her siblings. Worst of all, her doll was torn.

"What happened here?" Mrs. Eve picked up the wet bedding. She shook her head. "It must be your sisters."

Connie didn't know what to say.

"Sit in that corner and don't move," the woman instructed. Connie was so tired from all the work she'd done throughout the day that as soon as she sank to the floor, her head fell forward and she was asleep within minutes.

"Poor Lamb," Mrs. Eve whispered. "I'll do all I can to help you." And Mrs. Eve wrung the blanket and mattress dry, shaking her head as the water trailed on the floor. At least there was a small hole through which it seeped and disappeared into the wall. She carried the wet articles down to the kitchen, setting them in front of the fire. It was blazing and even as she dozed, waiting for her son to come and walk her home, she prayed for the little child sleeping on the floor upstairs.

Once everything was dry, she carried it all back up the stairs, walking with much difficulty because her joints ached. She quickly made up the bed and then half carried and half dragged the sleeping child, tucked her in and then kissed her on the forehead.

"Sleep well, child, and may tomorrow bring you better tidings than today." She picked up the destroyed doll and her lips twisted. "Only wicked children can do this much harm to their sister."

3
HOPING FOR BETTER

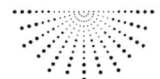

M*alone Manor – 1848*

From the small window in the attic, Connie could see the heavy, dark clouds, which looked ominous even this early morning.

Spring was here but the rains refused to let up. As she gazed outside, she wondered what her siblings were doing. They were probably sitting in front of the merry fire, sipping hot chocolate, or else they were in the schoolroom with Miss Owen. The governess lived in the small village just outside the estate and always came in very early. Connie didn't like her very much because she was stuck up and also, the little girl had noticed her father coming out of the schoolroom many times, and then Miss Owen would follow, straightening her clothes.

Connie's heart was filled with sorrow because Mrs. Eve had died two days ago. According to her son who had come to relay the news to Connie's parents the previous day, Mrs. Eve had gone to bed complaining of a headache and never woke up.

"What will happen to me?" the eight-year-old girl wept. For as long as the elderly woman had been the cook at the manor, Connie's mother's unkindness had lessened significantly. But now with no one to defend her Connie couldn't imagine what the days to come would be like. How would she survive in this household?

Twelve-year-old Abel was worried as he stood beside his father watching as Mrs. Eve's body was buried in the small public cemetery in the woods.

He knew that it was Mrs. Eve who had made life bearable for Connie at the manor. Because of the elderly woman, at least Connie had good clothes to wear, food to eat, and though her parents still whipped her from time to time, it was only when Mrs. Eve wasn't present. Now Mrs. Eve was dead and gone and Connie was once again alone in the house with her cruel parents and mischievous siblings.

If only his mother were still alive, Abel thought. He would have begged her to bring Connie to live with them. While his father was kind hearted and, once in a while, even intervened in the way Connie was treated by her parents, his stepmother was Mrs. Baker's good friend. It seemed like Mrs. Dawson, for he couldn't bring himself to think of her as 'Mama' or even 'Mrs. Pierson,' now controlled his father.

Abel shook his head, "No help from Mrs. Dawson," he muttered as he watched the grave diggers covering the grave. What would happen to Connie now?

Dinah Baker laughed unkindly as she sat in the living room with her husband. They were sharing a bottle of warmed port. It was one of the bottles from Mr. Malone's cellar and it was really good, unlike the usual cheap gin they had drunk before. Their situation had changed for the better, and it was time for them to live large.

"Won't you attend the burial," Mr. Baker had asked his wife, hence the laughter.

"I'd rather not have that old bat turning in her grave should I show up. There was no love lost between us and I can't say that I'm sorry she's dead. She was such a nosy woman and a busybody, too. Don't tell me that you'll miss her."

"My darling wife," Mr. Baker left his seat and joined his wife on the couch. "Her wages are what I'm most interested in."

Mrs. Baker frowned slightly, adjusting her position as she poured out more port in their glasses. "What do her wages have to do with anything?"

"Mrs. Eve was the highest-paid servant on this estate, and it will be a waste for that money to go nowhere. Now that she's dead and gone, what do you think will happen to the wages she used to earn? What if you tell Mr. Blackwell that you need to employ another cook?"

"The money still won't come to us, Gerald, and you can stop dreaming about that," his wife said impatiently. "I had already thought about doing that, but Mr. Blackwell is too shrewd to fall for that."

"What if you told him that you were ready to employ someone, and I take Mrs. Eve's place? Not to work, of course, but we could pretend that you have employed another cook."

Mrs. Baker laughed out loud, "Mr. Blackwell knows who you are, Gerald. What's more, you know that he never releases the servants' wages to me or anyone else. He insists on paying each one directly, so the moment you show up in his office or he comes here to pay wages, he will know the truth. Don't you wonder that those horrible stablemen talk down at us all the time? It's because they are not paid by us, or else they would behave. Mr. Blackwell has turned the servants against us, and I can't even get rid of those who irk me without incurring his wrath and displeasure."

"We have to find someone who will do the work, collect the wages and then bring the money to us."

"That might not work because Mr. Blackwell made it clear that he was the one who hired and also terminated the services of all servants on this estate. He would never accept just anybody to come and work here."

The two sat in thought for a while; then Mr. Baker smiled. "What about your friend, Mrs. Dawson? You could ask her to take Mrs. Eve's place, and then when she gets the wages, we can share them with her. Since she already lives on the estate, I don't think Blackwell will object."

"But will Anita Dawson be willing to work in the kitchen? Her husband Joel Pierson is one of the stablemen and her stepson Abel has also been receiving a small stipend from Mr. Blackwell to help around the estate. She may be poor but she's comfortable, and I doubt that she will want to lift a finger to work for us. Besides, I don't think she can even cook."

"She doesn't have to cook or clean. We have Connie to do that and one of the other maids can help her. What we can tell Mrs. Dawson is that we need a mature person to supervise the girls in the kitchen and she doesn't have to lift a finger. All she will do is to oversee everything they do. In that way even if Mr. Blackwell comes to check up on whatever is going on he will find her present."

"That nasty man should just drop dead," Dinah exclaimed angrily. "We live in a house that is full of very pricy items we could sell so we can have money. But no, that other wicked man's will stated that nothing should be sold, so Mr. Blackwell has to come and inspect the house items every week just to make sure we haven't sold anything."

"The vases are breakable. We could sell one and tell him that the children, well, Connie broke it."

But his wife shook her head, "You remember what happened to the vase that was in Mr. Malone's bedchamber? The one we sold to Henry Pitcher?"

"Yes, and we told Mr. Blackwell that Connie had broken it and got away with the lie."

"No, we didn't," Dinah looked at him with disgust on her face. "Mr. Blackwell insisted on seeing the shards of the broken vase and wouldn't release the monthly stipend until I showed him the pieces. Henry wasn't happy when he had to break the vase so Mr. Blackwell would release the money to me. I had to appease him by paying him back all his money."

"That man is really a pain in the neck."

"If we want to get money from him then we have to think of doing it in some other way, not by selling any of the precious items in this house."

"Don't worry, my pet," Gerald patted her arm. "You talk with Mrs. Dawson and let us plan this together."

"What if she tells her husband? You know that Joel Pierson was a good friend of Mr. Malone's and he could then tell Mr. Blackwell and we'll get into more trouble."

Mr. Baker was shaking his head, "You can be sure that Mrs. Dawson won't tell her husband anything. The woman likes to live large and competes with you, yet her husband is just a stableman. She'll definitely jump at the chance of making some free money."

"But you realise that Mr. Blackwell won't pay her as much as Mrs. Eve because she's a new employee. Mrs. Eve had been with Mr. Malone for years."

"I know that, but we need the money. Whatever we can get from that Blackwell fellow will be good enough. Just talk to your friend and get her to help us in this."

"I'll try but I'm not promising anything."

Connie was surprised to find Abel's stepmother in the kitchen a few days later. Too afraid to ask the woman what she was doing there, Connie picked up the broom and started sweeping the kitchen, aware of the woman's eyes following her every move.

"What's your name, Child?" Mrs. Dawson asked her.

"Constance, Ma'am."

"Why are you up this early and sweeping the kitchen? Shouldn't one of the maids be doing it? Isn't that why they have been employed in this house?"

The comment troubled Connie but she knew better than to respond to it. The last time she had responded to a similar comment by one of the maids, the girl had told her mother about it and trouble had been the result. No, she had to be careful about the servants in this house.

"It's not too early to clean the house, Ma'am," the eight-year-old said. "Breakfast needs to be served early because Miss Owen, the governess, likes to start the school lessons early."

"So, when you're done here you'll join your brothers and sisters in the school room?"

"Only if Miss Owen calls me in," Connie said, even as she knew that such would never happen. Miss Owen was under instructions from her parents to never let Connie share in the educating of her siblings. And since Connie had once caught Miss Owen being embraced by her father, the two of them didn't get along. So the woman would never do anything to help or go out of her way to be pleasant to Connie.

Connie finished sweeping and then took the rubbish to the pit at the back of the stable. The day was getting lighter, and she could at least see where she was going. She could hear the pigs squealing in the sty and hoped that nothing was attacking them. There were many wolves and foxes around because of the large forest surrounding the estate, and the wild animals often stole into pigsty or chicken run and caused a lot of havoc.

As she turned to walk back to the house, Abel hailed her, and she was startled since he had appeared out of nowhere.

"You scared me," she told him, putting a hand over her heart. Dawn was just breaking, and she could see his face clearly.

"I'm sorry for that but I needed to see you this early," he said, looking furtively around them.

"Why?"

"I found out that my stepmother is now working in your house. Don't talk much to her."

"Why not?" Connie thought about the woman she'd left in the kitchen. "She looks friendly enough."

"Mrs. Dawson and your mother are very good friends, and if you tell her anything, she will tell your mother. And then you'll be in trouble."

"Then what do I say when she asks me any questions?"

"Give her vague answers, and she will soon leave you alone. She and I don't get along, but I try to be cordial to her for my father's sake, and so should you. But don't trust her, not for a single moment."

"Thank you," once again there was squealing from the pigsty. "Abel would you check on the pigs? They have been squealing and making noise for a while now. Just be careful that it isn't a wolf or fox in there attacking them."

"All right, I'll do that. Do you want to come with me?"

Connie shook her head. "I need to go and start making breakfast before Mama wakes up." And with a slight nod, she was gone.

Abel walked to the sty, looking out for any wild animals. There were none, but he found that one of the sows had dropped a litter of six piglets and they were the ones doing all the squealing.

"You have done well, Mother Pig," he said. He smiled as the six piglets seemed to run around his ankles. Connie would really love them.

He recalled the first time he'd taken her to see the chicks in the hen run. Connie had been so excited and ignored all the pecking of the mother hens as she picked up the small chicks and held them close. And her eyes had glowed when she saw the new calves and foals that had been born. The girl was so full of life, and he liked showing her new things.

"Connie will really love you," but even as he played with the piglets his eyes were on the large sow, which seemed to be closely watching her little ones even as she lay on the ground breathing heavily.

Connie slipped back into the house and made her way to the hearth where she stoked the fire. Mrs. Dawson was nowhere to be found, and she merely shrugged and went on preparing breakfast. She was peeling a large pile of potatoes while seated on the floor when she noticed that someone had come into the kitchen. She tensed, expecting to see her father because those were heavy footsteps. But when the person came round the table, she noticed that he was a stranger.

"Who are you and what are you doing seated on the cold floor this early morning?" The man looked really stern and Connie wondered who he was. She'd never seen him before and wondered what he was doing in their house very early in the morning. "Didn't you hear what I asked you?"

"My…" But before she could say anything more her mother rushed into the kitchen.

4
PRAYERS IN THE NIGHT

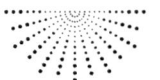

"Connie! What do you think you're doing?" Mrs. Baker asked, taking the large knife from her hands. Connie flinched when she thought her mother was about to strike her. It was a very fast reflex, but the stranger noticed it and his eyes narrowed.

"Mr. Blackwell," Connie was surprised to hear the note of deference in her mother's voice. "You know how children like to help around the kitchen and this one more than the others," she laughed, giving Connie a broad smile, which didn't reach her eyes. "Connie dear, why don't you run along to your room? I'll come by to check up on you," and she pushed the child past the stranger. Then she closed the kitchen door, shutting Connie out.

Something was going on with her mother and the stranger, and as Connie walked back to her attic room, there was a puzzled look on her face. She sat on the bed and looked around the small room.

While Mrs. Eve had still been alive, she'd done her best to make Connie's room very homely and had even put a bolt across the door. Well she hadn't done it herself, but she'd asked Mr. Joel, Abel's father, to do it so Connie would be safe. Connie smiled sadly; she would miss the elderly woman who had made her life bearable in this house.

Recalling what had just happened down in the kitchen a few minutes ago, the girl frowned. No one ever woke up as early as she did, and she knew that the stranger must have shocked her mother with his unexpected visit. The last thing she'd been expecting was to see her mother being even a little cordial to her. The stranger must be someone very important for her mother to become so flustered and send her away from the kitchen without her completing her duties.

She shrugged, lying back and pulling the covers over her head and was soon asleep.

∼

"Something happened in the house today," Connie told Abel when she met him at the woodshed later that afternoon. She'd gone to get some more wood and found him chopping up some logs.

"What happened?" He paused and wiped the sweat from his face.

"After you left to check on the pigs, I went to the house to prepare breakfast. As I was peeling the potatoes, a strange man came to the kitchen and looked at me in a funny way. He asked me what I was doing in the kitchen that early."

"Did he frighten you?"

Connie tilted her head slightly then shook her head. "No, he looked angry for some reason."

"So, what did you tell him?"

"Nothing! The moment I opened my mouth to talk to him, Mama came running into the kitchen, and she looked very troubled. She sent me to my attic room, and I fell asleep. A few minutes later she woke me up and took me to one of the locked-up rooms and told me that from today I was to sleep in there. And it's one of the really nice rooms."

"Have you ever seen the man before?"

"No, but I think Mama knows him very well. It was really surprising because she then brought the man to my new bedroom and told him that I have always slept in there. It is a pretty room with a very comfortable bed. If I didn't know any better, I would think Mama was going out of her way to appease the man."

"That is indeed surprising," Abel said. "And where was Mrs. Dawson?"

"That's the funny thing, I didn't find her in the kitchen and haven't seen her the whole day. Maybe the stranger frightened her away, too. His name is Mr. Blackwell; I heard Mama calling him that before she sent me out of the kitchen."

"Well, as long as that stranger doesn't bother you, just leave things well alone."

∽

For the next few weeks, Connie got respite from her mother and siblings because they avoided her, and she was free to come and go as she wished. Miss Owen found her walking toward the living room and smiled at her. Connie had never seen a smile on the woman's face, at least not directed toward her, and she was quite puzzled. And as for her father, she rarely saw him. It seemed as if everyone in the house was going out of their way to avoid her. She longed to see the man who had made things better for her in the house. But who would she ask about him since everyone was avoiding her?

She cooked and cleaned, helped by the remaining maid and even served food, yet no one criticized or insulted her, and she wondered what was going on. Abel's mother appeared once in a while but not daily. And on the days that Mrs. Dawson came to the house she seemed to be alert as if expecting something to happen.

"It's really odd," Connie told Abel one day. "No one is talking to me or even hitting me. And the other day, Miss Owen came to ask me if I wanted to have lessons in the schoolroom or in my bedchamber. You could have knocked me over with a feather, because the woman has never said more than two words to me ever since she joined this household."

"Isn't that a good thing?"

"I'm just afraid that it is just a brief respite before they start mistreating me all over again."

"Or maybe they have all changed and are trying to be nice."

"Maybe," Connie said thoughtfully.

"You should be happy now that no one is scolding you."

Connie wanted to be happy, but something didn't quite feel right. It was as if her family was waiting for something significant to happen, and then they would go back to being the same mean people all over again.

But perhaps what astonished her most was when her mother began insisting that she should take all meals with them. She had brought food to the dining room and was on her way back to the kitchen when her mother stopped her.

"Connie, sit here," her mother pulled out a chair for her, but she was afraid to sit in it. What if it was a trap like what had happened on Christmas Day two years ago?

"Mama, can I just eat in the kitchen?" she said with a trembling voice, not wanting to look at her father or siblings who were watching her.

"No," her mother actually touched her, ignoring the fact that Connie flinched. "From today and onward we will all eat together as a family."

And Connie was surprised that a new cook and two new maids were added to the household. She was no longer required to do any work in the house. What was going on?

∼

Seasons came and went, and the manor was silent as there was no quarrelling, and Connie was even allowed into the school room. The children were growing, and it soon became apparent that Connie was turning out to be a very beautiful girl. Even at the young age of twelve she was stunning and many times she found her sisters looking at her with something like anger in their eyes. But they didn't say anything mean to her, and she soon learned to ignore their pouting.

All this was going through Abel's mind as he walked to the woodshed from the stable. His stepmother had become very difficult to deal with, and he'd started spending his nights in the stables. There was a small room at the far end of the stable which was used as a storeroom for rakes and rope, and he'd made it comfortable for his use. His father didn't seem at all bothered that he wasn't spending nights at home, and Abel knew that his parent was relieved because of less tension in the house as a result of his absence. He also knew that his stepmother was always angry because she was no longer allowed to go to the manor. A new cook and two maids had come to work there, and Mrs. Baker told her that her services were no longer required.

"Father, what are you doing here?" he was surprised to find his father inside the manor's large woodshed. "You're not supposed to be chopping wood in this shed."

Joel frowned at his son, "I don't understand what you're asking me. Who do you think cuts down the trees in the forest and brings the logs here? Or do you think they just chop themselves down?"

Abel felt a little foolish when his father put it like that.

Joel chuckled at the expression on his son's face. "I see what you're doing here," he wagged a finger at him. "You think that because you're now sixteen you can do all the work alone? There's still some strength in these bones yet."

"Yes Pa," Abel didn't want his father to know that this was where he and Connie met for their long talks every day. His father wouldn't understand the kind of relationship they had, which even when Abel himself thought about it was quite puzzling. How did one explain the deep and growing feelings that a sixteen-year-old boy had for a soon to be twelve-year-old girl? Always at the back of his mind was the decision he'd come to years ago when he first met Connie. That he would work hard when he grew up, and then he would marry her.

"Come and help me because winter is coming soon, and we want there to be enough wood in the manor."

"Yes Pa."

∼

For the first time in twelve years Connie had a very different Christmas. She got a new dress and shoes and even a present under the Christmas tree. Her parents gave her a doll with a complete dollhouse and she wanted to laugh. This was the toy she'd desired when she was six years old when they had first come to live in the manor, but it had been given to Mary and Anne. If her parents had asked her what gift she wanted for Christmas, she would have told them that all she wanted were books to read. But since they didn't ask her, she didn't say anything, merely thanking them for their thoughtful present. Even though the doll was new, she didn't like it much because she felt like it was a forced present. She preferred her patched up ragdoll that had belonged to Mrs. Eve's granddaughter. After Mary and Anne had ripped it apart, Mrs. Eve had patched it up and it now had a prominent place on her pillow and surprisingly, no one said anything about it.

On Christmas Day in the morning the family gathered in the living room and Connie was allowed to be present, unlike all the other years when her place was in the kitchen. Her father was looking at her in a way that made her slightly uncomfortable.

"Come here, Connie," he said, holding out his arms. But she took a step backward and away from him as her siblings went on unwrapping their own presents. The last time her father had told her to come to him had been on Christmas Day six years ago, and when she did, he'd been so unkind. "Connie, I have a good present for you," he said.

"You already gave me the doll and dollhouse last night," she said in a trembling voice. "Thank you."

"No, my dear child, I have another present for you. Come and get it." But she shook her head and slipped behind Mrs. Bridges the new cook. Something else that surprised her was that her parents and siblings seemed to be afraid of Mrs. Bridges in the same way they had feared Mrs. Eve. In her heart, Connie called the woman her guardian angel. And now as Connie slipped behind her, Mrs. Bridges gave her father a defiant look, as if daring him to come closer and get her.

There was an awkward moment before her mother laughed, and it sounded very false in Connie's ears. "Leave the child alone," she said. "Just put the present under the tree and she'll take it later."

Connie sighed with relief that she didn't have to get close to her father. He made her very uncomfortable. At dinnertime, she was very careful to sit as far away from him as possible and was glad that Mrs. Bridges was there. The older woman reminded her of Mrs. Eve and also looked out for her. Even though her family were mysteriously cordial to her, Connie still didn't trust them.

Twelve years of being mistreated didn't all just go away because of the kindness of a few months. No, she shook her head slightly, there had to be something else going on that made her family mellow toward her. This wasn't normal, and she was very sure it wouldn't last. So, much as she enjoyed the positive attention, she was still very wary.

∼

"I don't like that horrible Mrs. Bridges living in this house. It's been two years now, and she doesn't seem to be leaving," Connie heard her mother telling her father. She'd been passing the study, which her father used as an office, on her way to her bedroom when she heard them mention her guardian angel's name and stopped to listen. "Two whole years, and she doesn't seem like she will be leaving any time soon."

"You have to understand that we have to put up with Mrs. Bridges because of that Blackwell fellow," her father said. "Or else he will stop our monthly allowance. He was the one who brought her here and now we have to just grin and bear her presence, even though it annoys me greatly."

"That man," Mrs. Baker said in an angry tone, "He really tries my patience, and I just wish there was a way of getting rid of him and all the lackeys he foists on us and who are his spies."

"For as long as he holds the purse strings, we have to put up with him and his lackeys as you call them. But don't worry about him, my love, just another nine years until she turns twenty-one and then we'll be rid of all of them once and for all. We have come this far, let's just keep holding on."

"When you say it like that, it makes sense. But nine years is still a long time to put up with all this nonsense."

"Well, Mr. Malone's Will stipulates that when she turns eighteen, she can get married and then her husband can control her inheritance."

"That's still another six years to go."

"But it gives us time to make plans and find a husband for her, a man who will obey us and do whatever we tell him. That's the only way we'll get the better of all of them, starting with that Blackwell fellow. Once he marries her and gains control of her inheritance, we'll quickly deal with him, so he won't ever be a problem to us again."

"We have to be very careful so that our plans are not discovered by anyone."

Connie tiptoed away from the door wondering who her parents were talking about and feeling sorry for the person because it was clear that ill was intended for her.

∽

On Connie's fourteenth birthday, her mother threw her a party and even had Mrs. Bridges bake her a large cake. There were many presents for her, even some from her siblings, but she was still wary. The only hitch on the day was that Mrs. Bridges said she had to travel to London to visit her daughter who had just had a baby.

"I wish I could take you with me, my little lamb," Mrs. Bridges told her as she was leaving. She kissed her and Connie saw something like sorrow in her eyes.

"But you'll be back soon, won't you?"

"Yes," but Mrs. Bridges avoided her eyes. Connie soon forgot about the sad look in her guardian angel's eyes when she saw the large cake and the presents that were meant for her.

But all the goodwill changed later that night. As she lay in bed wide awake, just thinking about the past few years, she wondered if she should just accept that her parents had changed. But she also felt that it was because of Mrs. Bridges who was like a real mother to her now. What would happen to her if Mrs. Bridges never returned and left her forever like Mrs. Eve had done? Would life go back to the hell it had been before?

Yes, her parents and siblings had changed toward her, but she always felt that they were forcing themselves to be good to her because of Mrs. Bridges.

The household was so quiet she could hear the slightest noise. And she thought she heard someone tiptoe past her room and then return. The footsteps then stopped outside her bedroom and she felt the hairs on the back of her neck rising.

For some reason there was no key in the keyhole and the bolt had been removed just earlier that day, but she didn't know who had done it. Feeling unsafe, she slipped out of the bed and ran to the corner of her bedchamber where she crouched low and waited to see what would happen. She wished Mrs. Bridges was around because her bedchamber was just across the hallway from Connie's.

The door opened slowly, and her heart was pounding so hard that she was afraid that whoever it was would hear her. Because she loved looking at the full moon, she hadn't drawn her curtains that night, so she was able to make out the figure that approached her bed. It was her father, and she put a hand over her mouth to prevent herself from gasping loudly.

"Come on, Connie, you know you want this," he whispered, raising the blankets and slipping into her bed.

Connie heard angry footsteps and light suddenly flooded the bedroom.

"What is going on here?" Her mother stood in the doorway holding a lamp. "Gerald, what are you doing in Connie's bed?"

Her father scrambled out of her bed. "I heard her screaming and came to comfort her."

"You're a liar," Dinah spat out. "I wasn't sleeping yet and heard you leave our bedroom. At least I would have thought that you would sneak out of bed to visit one of the maids. Tell me the truth; what were you doing in Connie's bed? If you don't, I'll set this whole house on fire and burn it to the ground. Then we'll see which other bedroom you'll be creeping into with no roof over your head."

"It wasn't my fault. She told me to come to her bedroom when it was dark. I always told you that she is trouble, but you wouldn't listen. It's not my fault."

"And where is she now?" Dinah screeched, rushing towards the bed and tossing the quilt and blankets aside. "Where is that detestable girl?"

Connie was glad that their attention wasn't on her and she slid behind the thick drapes and stayed very still. She couldn't believe that her own father had crept into her room in the middle of the night and slipped into her bed, clearly intending evil for her.

Mrs. Bridges had told her to be careful about allowing a man to touch her because they had ill intentions. That was the reason she had personally fixed a bolt on Connie's door. But then someone had removed it this evening, and it was looking like it was her father who had done it so he could gain entry. She trembled when she thought about what might have happened had she been sleeping when he came in.

"I notice that you and that Abel boy are getting very close. You are only fourteen and he is eighteen. Be careful about letting him or any other man touch you or get into your bed."

"Why?"

"It's a foolish question but I'll answer you. Only married people should sleep in the same bed or else you will soon find yourself with a baby. And the man will hurt you so much in the process. Be very careful of every man."

And she wondered why her own father would want to lie in her bed. She wanted to stand up and tell her mother that it was her father who had come in without any invitation, but she held her peace.

"You are going to tell me the truth, Gerald," Dinah walked toward him and he fled with her in hot pursuit.

Connie wasn't able to sleep for the rest of the night, and in the morning her mother burst into her bedroom, dragging her out of bed. She then proceeded to grab all the nice clothes and shoes as well as all the presents they had bought her and carried them to the pit at the back of the house, then set them on fire. Connie watched silently as the presents that had been bought for her, including her dollhouse from two years ago, followed her clothes into the fire.

"You will never set foot in this room again," Dinah told Connie coldly, dragging her by the ears up to the attic. "This was your room before, and you won't ever leave it."

∽

"I couldn't believe my eyes," Dorcas, one of the maids, was telling Celine the other maid. Connie had felt hungry and decided to slip down to the kitchen to see if she could get something to eat. Now that all grace was over, she knew that she would no longer be welcomed at the dining table. "That woman grabbed the poor girl's clothes and shoes and threw them in the pit. Everything went up in flames and I'm sure Mrs. Baker even wished to push the girl herself into the fire to burn with her stuff. If Mrs. Bridges had been here I don't think she would have done that."

"But Mrs. Bridges is gone, and I pity Connie. But why would her mother burn her clothes and everything else?"

"Because Mr. Baker has his eye on the girl."

"What?" Celine said in a shocked voice. "That girl is only fourteen years old, and besides she is his daughter."

"Well that man is not her birth father."

"That's a lie."

"No, Celine, I speak the truth," Dorcas said. "At the time Mrs. Dinah was getting married to Mr. Baker, she was already heavy with child and it wasn't his."

"How do you know all this?"

"People talk and besides, Mrs. Eve who worked here a few years ago was my relative and told my mother."

"So, Connie's father is somewhere out there?"

"Yes, but you can never tell anyone. This is our secret," and they fell silent.

But Connie had heard enough, and so much finally made sense to her. No wonder her father, no, Mr. Baker, didn't like her and did everything to hurt her. She wasn't his daughter and therefore he felt he could be as cruel as he wanted.

∼

"We don't need a cook," Mrs. Baker told Mr. Blackwell who was looking at her coldly. "Mrs. Bridges made life very difficult for all of us."

"So, who will do the cooking at the manor?"

"We have Celine and Dorcas and they can manage all the work. Just increase their wages to cover the extra duties and I know they will work hard."

"If you think that's the right thing to do, then so be it."

Mrs. Dinah walked out of Mr. Blackwell's office with a sinister smile on her face. She had managed to get rid of Mrs. Bridges by framing her for theft since she knew Mr. Blackwell was very strict about such matters. Now she could control the household like she had always wanted to and no fourteen-year-old girl was going to stand in her way.

"Connie, come here at once," she called out to her when she got home.

"Yes Mama," Connie came running and Mrs. Baker gave her such a look of hatred that the girl was shocked.

Mrs. Baker grabbed her and forced her to the floor and then proceeded to shave off her hair. "You can now go," she said in satisfaction as the child wept over her beautiful locks. "Mary and Anne, come and see what this one looks like."

Mary, Anne, Grant and John ran into the living room, and when they saw Connie's shorn head, they laughed, teasing her mercilessly.

"Mama, she looks so ugly," thirteen-year-old Mary said. "She used to boast that her hair was longer than mine and she was prettier."

"Look at her now," Mrs. Baker jeered. "You, my girls, are the most beautiful young things in the world, and there is no one who can ever come close to you. Everyone else is just jealous of you, including this foolish girl."

Connie carried her hair in her hands and left the living room. She was crying so hard that she didn't see Mr. Baker in the corridor.

"What is going on," he asked, reaching out to touch her.

But Connie struggled and managed to get away, running through the kitchen and out of the house.

5
LAMENTATIONS FOR LOVE

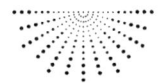

"Connie, you can pretend all you want that things are all right, but you can't deceive me," there was an intensity in Abel's eyes that unnerved her. He'd found her sweeping the stables, which she wasn't supposed to do, since that was his work. But her mother had told her to clean the place, and Abel had heard her. "Please talk to me and tell me the truth." He wondered why she was wearing an old woollen bobble hat over her head.

"It's nothing," the fourteen-year-old sniffed. She was in anguish as she recalled what she'd overheard Celine and Dorcas discussing. No wonder her mother could barely stand her, and as for Mr. Gerald, she was terrified of him. And then her mother had shaved her head and she knew that she looked very ugly, her sisters had said so. She didn't want Abel to see her bald head because he would be repulsed.

"Connie?"

She dashed her tears away and as she bent down to pick up the broom, the hat fell off her head.

"Connie, what happened to your hair?" Abel was so shocked that he was speechless for a few minutes. "Who did that to you?"

"It's nothing."

"No, please don't say it's nothing when you're crying, and someone has shaved your beautiful hair off. Where did you throw your locks?"

Connie was crying as she pulled them out of her pocket.

"Give them to me and I'll keep them for you."

"Why?" But even as she asked him, she handed over the thick tresses to him. He would keep them safe for her. She didn't know why, but that thought brought her a little happiness after the terrible time she'd had in the past two days.

"Because your hair is beautiful, and I want to look at it all the time."

"But I'm ugly now," she wept.

"Connie listen to me; you will never be ugly to me. Even if they cut your hair off and pluck your eyes out of your face, you are still the most beautiful girl in the world." He held out his hand for the bobble hat. "Give that to me. You don't have to hide your head because you are very beautiful," and he took it from her, then stuffed the hair in it. "Wait here," he entered the stable and was gone for a short time and returned empty handed. "Your hair is safe with me now. But as I said, it's not only hair that makes you beautiful, Connie. You have so much else going for you."

"You're just saying that to make me feel better," she blew her nose at the edge of her long skirt.

"No," Abel drew closer and raised her chin with his finger, "Look at me, Connie." And she did. "You are so beautiful and not just on the outside, but inside as well. That is the true beauty."

"I'm not beautiful like Mary and Anne."

"No, you're not," and she paled but he hurried to reassure her. "You may not have beauty such as theirs because with them it is just on the outside and their hearts are dark. One day what I'm saying will make sense to you. But just know this, you are the most beautiful girl in the world to me and I will never stop saying that for the rest of my life."

Connie suddenly felt very self-conscious when she saw a strange light in Abel's eyes. She could feel the heat from his body, and she felt something like butterflies in her stomach. Recalling Mrs. Bridges' words about never letting a man get too close to her, she pulled away and picked up the broom.

"I have to go back inside the house before Mama begins calling out for me."

"Connie..." Abel called out softly as he touched her hand, willing her not to leave just yet. But she shook his hand off and hurried back to the house. Celine and Dorcas had left that morning, looking at her with so much pity in their eyes. She had a feeling that they wouldn't be returning, and as for Mrs. Bridges, it was clear the woman was also gone for good.

Mary and Anne were in the kitchen and they were causing a mess. They didn't seem to care that she had cleaned the house just that morning.

"Why are you spilling milk all over the counter and floor," she asked them, taking a cloth to wipe the mess.

"Why are you spilling milk all over the counter and floor," Mary mimicked while Anne deliberately tipped the jar and spilled even more milk. "Who are you to question us when this is our father's house? You're nothing more than a leech and you should be ashamed of yourself. Just look at how ugly you are with your hairless head."

"Why do you hate me so much?" Connie whispered. "You're my sisters, and I love you, but you treat me so badly." She truly loved all her siblings and desired more than anything to be close with them. "What did I ever do to you?"

"Mama," Anne called out. "Connie has spilled all the milk."

"What did you say?" Dinah rushed into the kitchen and Connie's heart sank when she saw the look on her mother's face. This was trouble and her sisters were clearly enjoying her pain.

"Connie spilt the milk and then she talked back at Mary," Anne piped. "She said me and Mary are so ugly and she doesn't want to be our sister." Grant and John entered the kitchen after their mother, and Connie could see the malicious glee in her siblings' eyes. Not even one of them ever defended her to their mother and she bowed her head, waiting for the punishment that was about to be unleashed on her.

Dinah pulled Connie roughly.

"What is going on here?" Gerald entered the kitchen from the outside door. He'd been looking at the cows in the barn and then decided to return to the house. Abel was behind him but didn't come close to the house. He knew that Connie was in trouble and more than anything, he wished he could push his way into the house and save her.

"This stupid girl spilt all the milk," Dinah said. "What kind of a person is this we're breeding in our house?"

Connie had had enough of all the pain and everything just seemed to well up within her. "Take me to my father," she cried out and there was sudden pin drop silence in the kitchen.

"You want to go to your father?" Dinah's voice was menacing, but Connie didn't care anymore.

"Yes, because it's clear that you don't want me here," she wiped her nose with the back of her sleeve. "Why do you hate me so much? If you don't want me here, then take me to my father."

"Mary, take your brothers out to the yard," Dinah said.

"Yes Mama," and the four of them left the house, running into Abel who followed them.

Abel heard shouts coming from the kitchen and his heart nearly broke. Mary and Anne were laughing as were their brothers. He walked up to them and looked at them with anger in his eyes. The two girls liked to flirt with him and indeed with all men who came to the house, and they batted their eyelashes at him, but he curled his lip in disgust.

"I know that it's the two of you who have caused trouble for Connie," he told them as their faces paled. "You can laugh now as your sister, but one day, you will also know the pain of being treated as badly as you've always treated Connie."

"Don't talk to us about that useless girl," Mary found her voice. "She is so ugly with her shorn head. Mama says no man will ever look at her again."

Abel smiled at them coldly, "You call her useless and ugly because you're jealous of her."

"What? In those tattered clothes and the bald head that looks like that of a new-born baby?"

"Yes Anne, even in her tattered clothes and shorn head, Connie is more beautiful than ten of you. You may be decked in all your fine clothes but let me tell you something, you will never hold a candle to Connie, not even the tiniest one. You're just ten and twelve years old and yet you are so full of bitterness and jealousy against your own sister. I really pity the two of you."

"Go away," Mary took her shoe off and threw it at him but missed.

"I'm going because I don't want to breathe in the same foul air as the two of you. But before I go just know that one day the two of you and your brothers will pay for all this. I feel sorry that such small girls like you have such dark hearts. You've been taught to hate your own sister who loves you and does everything for you. But one day you will need her, and I pray that I will be there to see your shame when that time comes."

Mary scooped a handful of dust and flung it at Abel. It splattered all over his shirt, and he looked down at the mess and then back at her with pity in his eyes. He shook his head and then turned around to walk away. Then he stopped and turned around again to face them as they stood there staring at him.

"Just know this, everything you do on this earth, you do for yourself," he said. "When you do good, then one day you'll reap good in abundance. But as the two of you and your brothers have decided to sow evil while still very young, your days to come are going to be filled with so much evil."

The two girls merely laughed at Abel, insulting him as he walked back to the stables.

The cries had died down and all was silent once again in the kitchen. It was an eerie kind of silence and Abel wanted to rush in and find out whatever was happening, but Gerald was a bully, and the last thing he wanted was to get Connie into more trouble.

So he entered the stable and began cleaning as he'd been doing before the trouble had started. His jerky movements seemed to agitate the horses because his trowel was knocking hard against the stalls. They began neighing and stamping their hooves and he knew that he needed to calm down. It wouldn't do any good for the horses to get fidgety and begin to stamp harder. But he wished he could find out what was going on in the house. It was too quiet. Then a dreadful thought entered his mind. What if Connie was dead?

A few days ago, he'd overhead his stepmother telling his father that Mrs. Baker had reported Mrs. Bridges to Mr. Blackwell because she'd stolen a vase from the house and the woman had lost her position. And just that morning the other two maids had told Randy that they were no longer working in the house. According to the one called Dorcas, Mrs. Baker had woken up that morning and told them that their services were no longer required at the manor. So it was now up to Connie to do all the work in the house.

She had been right in suspecting that her family's gracious behaviour toward her was only for a short while. And now that the grace was over, the abuse had returned with a vengeance. He felt so agitated and wished he could go in and see her.

∽

In the tirade of lies and questions that her parents were throwing at her, Connie quietly prayed.

"Dear Lord, take my soul and give me peace at last."

"You want to go to your father, isn't it?" Gerald's hand swung round and struck her. Connie lost her footing and sprawled towards to stove, reaching helplessly out to stop her fall. Her bald head hit the iron edging and in a moment, and she caught her leg awkwardly in the grillwork trying to save herself. Connie lay still on the stone foor. A pool of blood gathered by her head, her leg twisted.

Mrs. Baker pushed her husband aside and stared down at the still figure on the floor and felt panic well up within her. "Is she dead?"

"She's only pretending," Gerald said as he kicked her motionless body. But Connie didn't move and just lay there, her skin turning white. There was blood all over the floor and Mr. Baker suddenly snapped out of the frenzy that had taken over his senses. "She is lying so still," he raised his eyes to his wife. "Why won't this girl wake up?"

"I think she's dead," Mrs. Baker said. "Why did you have to hit her so hard? What kind of trouble have you brought to us?" She glared at him. "How will we explain this to the children and other people when they ask about Connie? What is wrong with you?"

"Don't blame me, woman," Gerald snarled back. "We're in this together and don't you forget it. Not a word to anyone or you'll see trouble like never before."

Dinah was frightened of her husband and nodded jerkily.

"Let's take the body to the attic and lock it there as we think of what to do."

"No," Mrs. Baker said sharply. "It will start decaying and the stench will be too much and we won't be able to stay in the house."

"Then what do you suggest we do? We don't have much time and the children could come back to the house any minute now and find her here. They will then talk to their friends and you can imagine the kind of trouble that will land on our doorstep."

"Let me think," Mrs. Baker paced the kitchen, quite shaken. Her hands were shaking, and she stuck them into her pockets. "Why can't you control your temper, you imbecile? Now there will be so much trouble. If the children see this, who knows who they will tell and what they will say? What about Mr. Blackwell?"

"Woman, stop blaming me and yet you were in this with me all through. We have to make sure that no one sees this body."

"But even if we get rid of this body, what will we tell the children when they ask where Connie is?"

Gerald twisted his lips, "It's simple. This silly girl wanted to go to her father. Tell them that she ran away to find her father. After all, they all heard her shouting that we should take her to her father and that's the story we'll tell anyone who asks about her."

Mrs. Dinah's face brightened. "Yes, we'll say that she ran away." Then her face fell. "Mr. Blackwell will never believe that story."

"Then it's up to you to make sure that he never comes by the house again. Do everything you can to keep him away. We can say that she decided to elope with some man. You saw how the girl liked to make eyes at men."

His wife gave him a piercing look and then shrugged. "You really think people will believe that a fourteen-year-old eloped with some man?"

"What other choice do we have but to convince them of that? Meanwhile what will we do with this body? We have to get rid of it. Clean up the blood quickly before the children come in. I don't want them to get traumatized when they see it."

"Wait," Mrs. Baker said. "The loft in the stable is empty. Let's put the body there until we decide on how to dispose of it."

"Good idea but the steps are really narrow and rickety. No one has used that loft in years."

"We have to do this fast before the children get hungry and come back to the house. Let me get an old quilt we can roll the body in and make it easy to carry."

"Quick then, we have no time to waste."

6

THE UNDESIRABLE ELEMENTS

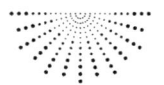

Never had Abel come close to hating anyone in his life like he did at that moment. Hiding in one of the horses' stalls, he watched as Mr. Gerald and Mrs. Dinah carried the thick quilt up the steps to the loft. He was sure that it was Connie's body and he let his tears flow. Why hadn't he rushed in to help her when she needed him? Now it was too late for him to do anything for her.

"No one will ever find the body there since no one goes to the loft," Mr. Gerald looked around as if he expected someone to emerge from the darkness. "After we move the horses out of the stable, we'll set the place on fire and the body will be burnt without a trace. It will then cover us."

"But we still have to find a place for the horses to be put first. We don't want them running away or being stolen. Mr. Blackwell would never stop blaming us for that. Let's just leave the body here for a day or two and then we can come and carry it away in the night. Instead of burning down the stable which will be a great loss to us, let's dig a grave in the woods and after two days we'll come and carry the body away for burial."

Abel waited until they had closed the loft door and left the stable. He sat in the stall for a long while, and when he was sure that no one would be coming back, he crept up the steps, tears still flowing down his face. After all the unkindness they had subjected Connie to over the years, they had finally killed her. He wished his father and stepmother were here so he could tell them what had happened. But they had travelled to Bristol to enjoy the sun.

And he didn't dare leave the stable because he was afraid the two wicked people who had killed Connie would come and carry her body away in his absence. No, he would just check on her and if she was really dead, he would wait for them to come for the body. Then he would follow them so he could see where they buried it and then he would report the matter to the village constable.

As he entered the dark loft, he thought he heard a soft moan. The sound startled him, and he stood still, his eyes getting accustomed to the darkness. Being careful not to make any frightening sounds, he crept to the small wooden window and opened it slightly to let the fading light in. It would soon be dark, and he wanted to make sure that Connie was really dead. It was a good thing that the window opened toward the fields so no one could see in from the house.

Then he rushed to the still form and unwrapped the quilt, nearly crying out loudly when he saw her. Her shorn head was a mess of blood, and he bowed his head, deep grief in his heart—and rage too.

"Dinah and Gerald," he hissed, "One day you will pay for this."

Connie moaned and Abel sobbed in relief. She was alive, but her breathing was laboured. He noticed the grotesque position of her left leg. He'd seen one of the horses with such an injury a few weeks ago. Connie's leg had been broken when she was roughly yanked from the kitchen floor and thrown into the quilt, and looked just like that poor horse.

Mr. Gerald, careless man that he was, had been riding Polka Dot, the horse Connie loved so much, and the animal didn't like him. He kept striking it and finally it stumbled and got its leg stuck into a hole. The leg had snapped and Mr. Gerald had told Abel's father to put the animal down. But his father had led the injured animal gently to the woods, pretending to be going to fulfil his master's wishes. Once there, however, Abel's father had made a splint and bound up the horse's leg.

"Pa, didn't Mr. Gerald say you should get rid of the horse? Why are you doing this?" Abel had asked. "Mr. Gerald said you should just shoot the horse."

"Son, I have worked as a stable man for over twenty years," his father had replied. "There are those times when yes, you have to put an animal down when it's injured. But this isn't one of those times. This horse has broken its leg, and we will treat it until it gets better. But if Mr. Gerald asks you, tell him I got rid of it as he had asked me to do."

And the treatment worked. A few days later, his father had sold the horse to a travelling salesman who promised to take very good care of it. He simply wanted to use it to carry his goods and said he wouldn't overload it. And that was the money his father and stepmother had used to travel to Bristol on holiday.

"Forgive me, Connie," Abel muttered as he felt her leg. It was her thigh bone that was broken, and the moment he touched it, Connie moaned and then fell silent once again.

"At least you're unconscious," he said. "So you won't feel the pain as I set your leg."

There were some pieces of wood down in the stable and he rushed to find them, grabbing an old shirt left by one of the other stablemen and returned to the loft. He ripped the shirt to make bandages and strips to use to bind the leg.

He'd watched his father carefully and did the same to Connie's leg. He then wiped the blood from her head and face, and as well as he could, made her comfortable.

"I will watch over you and protect you," he promised the still unconscious girl. "They won't hurt you again, not while I'm alive and watching."

∼

"I'm really worried about that body," Mr. Baker told his wife. They were in their bedroom and the children were all asleep.

"What should we do then?"

"Let's take the children away for a few days then I will return and organize how to dispose of the body." He made a sound of disgust. "The girl was trouble when she was alive, and even in death she gives us no peace."

"Calm down, my husband. Don't get agitated. We are well rid of her and she will never be a bother to us again."

"I'm still worried because of that body being in the loft. What if it starts to stink and someone decides to investigate? How will we explain things to the constable or coroner?"

Mrs. Baker smiled, "That's the reason your suggestion of taking the children away for a few days will work very well. We will say that the cursed girl ran away or rather we thought she did, but she must have hidden in the loft and met her death there."

"But how will we explain the wounds and bruises?"

"There are three people who work in the stables, four if you count that young boy who helps around here, Joel's son. When the body is found they will be the first suspects because they are always in the stable."

"You forget that Joel is away in Bristol with his wife, the two-faced woman who must have told Connie that I wasn't her father. I don't know why you had to tell her all our secrets. Now she can start blackmailing us, and we don't want anyone to know our secrets."

"And I thought she was my friend," Mrs. Dinah scowled. "I never expected that she would turn against us and even reveal the secret to Connie. She is a very dangerous woman, and I'm just glad that she is away. Let them return when all this is over. The constable can treat them like suspects and since the children don't know what is going on, they will be our best alibis and witnesses."

"Very well then, we'll go away and then I will return. But I can't be seen around here, or someone will get suspicious. Those stablemen, which you say are very insolent because we don't directly pay their wages, could cause us trouble."

"What about Joel's boy?"

Mr. Gerald shook his head, "I don't think that one will be any trouble. The boy has no sense in his head. It's the other two that I'm more worried about."

"Don't you worry about them," Mrs. Dinah said with confidence. "They are both drunkards and lazy oafs. It's Joel and his imbecile of a son who do all the work in the stables. In fact, we should just burn down the stable and then tell the police constable that it was those two drunks who set it on fire. Everyone knows that they often get into fights and cause a lot of havoc down at the tavern. Burning a stable when their masters are away is something they would do."

"Still, we need to get rid of the boy."

"That's very easy to do. All we have to do is tell him that we're selling the horses and his services on the estate are no longer required. We could even ask Henry Pitcher to give him work at his own stable."

Mr. Gerald frowned at his wife, "I don't trust that Henry Pitcher fellow and yet you seem to have a lot of doings with him. What is it the two of you discuss?"

Mrs. Baker laughed softly, "Is my husband perhaps jealous of a very innocent relationship? Mr. Pitcher is a harmless fellow, and I thought he was your very good friend. After all, you were the one who introduced him to this family. Weren't you very close at one point? I'm just being a good friend's wife to him."

"Let's not talk about that worthless fellow when we have more urgent matters to take care of. If we have to burn down the stable, then we need to find a place to keep the horses. Fifteen horses would need a large stable and plenty of fodder. Once we're rid of the stable and the body, we can then rebuild and bring them back."

Mrs. Dinah nodded slowly, "What if we asked our neighbours to keep the horses for us for a few days?"

"Don't you think it will look very suspicious if we asked our neighbours to take in our horses and then suddenly the stable burnt down? We need to come up with a very good explanation for asking for the neighbours' help."

"What if we said we were renovating the stable and needed to get the horses away for a short while? And if the stable burns down during the renovations, then no one will be suspicious and if all else fails, your friend Henry has a large stable because he sold all his horses. He could keep them for us."

Mr. Gerald smiled at his wife, "I like the way you think, Mrs. Baker," he approached the bed as she gave him a coy look. "We make a good team."

∽

Abel was worried about Connie and wished his parents were around. It was the second day after the traumatic experience, but she wasn't coming out of unconsciousness.

But at least she was breathing. He brought some warm water with a little salt in it and bathed her head, hands and face. He found some ointment at their cottage and applied it to her bruises. He prayed that Mr. and Mrs. Baker wouldn't think of coming to the loft until she got better.

When there was nothing more to be done for his patient, he left the loft, carefully shutting the door and bolting it from the outside. As he stepped out of the stable, he noticed that Mrs. Baker was working hurriedly in the kitchen and wondered what was going on. Randy came around and stood next to Abel.

"Mr. Randy, what is going on with Mrs. Baker? She seems to be in a great hurry."

"Mr. Baker and his wife are taking their children to Bath for a holiday. They are visiting some relatives there."

"Oh," Abel pursed his lips. "What about Miss Connie? Isn't she going with them? They can't leave her in this large house alone now that there are no servants working inside, that is, apart from us here at the stables."

Randy shook his head, "As I was harnessing the horses to the carriage, I overheard Mr. Baker telling Samuel that the girl ran away. Apparently, she no longer wanted to live here," Randy scratched his dirty beard. "I don't blame the little missy for running away. The way these people have been treating her," he shook his head. "But I feel like something is not quite right," but he shrugged and shuffled off, taking his foul odour with him and Abel wrinkled his nose.

So, these people were abandoning poor Connie because they thought she was already dead. None of them had gone up to the loft to check up on her, and for that, Abel was glad. He couldn't believe just how cruel people could be and to their own child. And after disposing of her, they were now running away. What if he hadn't been around? It was just as well they thought of him as being of no threat to them because of the way he acted when they were around. They called him a senseless imbecile, and he acted as if he really was one.

But he would be here for Connie and take care of her until she was well. Thankfully, Mr. Baker, though he felt like the lord of the manor, was afraid of the horses. And the animals didn't seem to like him at all. Actually, the only person the horses responded well to was Connie. No wonder the other four children didn't even want to learn how to ride.

All this was to his advantage because they never set foot too far into the stable. It was a large building with enough stalls to house twenty horses, but they currently had only fifteen of them. He had converted the last stall into a small room where he slept and also prepared meals for himself and now Connie.

Randy and Nick never ventured too far into the stable either. They were just too lazy to put any effort into anything that needed doing. For once, Abel was glad that his fellow workers were too lazy and always drunk. This was the perfect situation and he would do everything possible to make sure Connie recovered.

And then he would talk to her about running away together. Yes, he would take her out of this horrible place and make sure that her family never found her again. It didn't matter that she was just fourteen years old; she needed him to protect her from her family. This horrid family didn't deserve this sweet girl.

But he had to be careful because of her age. Her parents could create trouble if they caught up with them.

"Connie," he called out softly later as he raised her head and tried to feed her some chicken broth. Now that his master and mistress weren't here, he'd taken one chicken from the coop and slaughtered it, preparing tasty broth just like his mother had taught him. Abel really missed his mother at a time like this, and to his surprise, he also wished his father and Mrs. Dawson would come back.

It was really hard to feed Connie because she was not responsive. He spooned some broth into her mouth then held her nose. As she took a shuddering breath, she was forced to swallow the broth. It was hard going but he managed to feed her half a bowl.

"Connie, please wake up so you can eat and get better. Your life is in danger and I need to get you out of here. But you have to wake up."

But Connie remained comatose. He wiped her lips, placing her back on the floor. After covering her, he kissed her forehead and moved to the door. Much as he wanted to step out and return to his small room to sleep, he was worried about her. No, he would spend the night right here and watch over her.

"Sleep well, dear girl, and let's pray that you get better by tomorrow," he stretched himself across the doorway just in case anyone tried to come in. They would have to get through him to harm Connie. "You have to wake up, you just have to be better, Connie."

~

"Mrs. Bridges, what are you doing here?" Joel Pierson approached the elderly woman and stood over her. The woman put away her knitting needles and wool and looked up at him, frowning at the interruption. She'd been enjoying some peace and quiet at the beach while watching little children frolicking around and adults walking by. From the scowl on her face, Joel realised that the woman didn't want to be disturbed.

"What does it look like I'm doing?" The woman scowled at him. "This is the beach, and I am here for the sun. And what are you doing here?"

"My wife was having some trouble with her bones and the doctor recommended that I bring her to the beach for some sun and saltwater."

"Where is your good wife?"

"She is…" Joel looked around and then waved. "Here she is."

The two women smiled politely at each other. "If you're here in Bristol who is working at the manor?" Mrs. Dawson asked.

"Why don't you find out from your best friend?" Mrs. Bridges smiled thinly. "That woman is a very wicked person. And she hates that poor child with her whole heart and yet she is her mother."

"Don't talk about my friend like that," Mrs. Dawson said.

"Go and tell her if you want," Mrs. Bridges said. "See if I care. She has already done her worst, but one day she will get what is coming to her."

"You sound really bitter."

"No, Mr. Joel, I'm not bitter. I'm just angry that I lost my good position because the woman lied that I had stolen some vase from the house. Mr. Blackwell retained my wages to pay for the vase and the woman gloated. But one day...." she didn't finish her sentence. Instead she got to her feet, gathered her knitting and stashed it into her basket. "Have a good day, folks."

Later that afternoon as Mrs. Dawson was strolling through the shops, she bumped into Mrs. Bridges. "Please stop," she told the older woman who scowled at her.

"If you want to talk about your friend, I have nothing to say."

"No," Mrs. Dawson said. "I had time to think about what you said, and I think you were right."

"How do I know you're not just saying this?"

"Joel talked to me also and told me what Mrs. Baker has been doing to Connie. It's appalling, and I'm ashamed that I haven't been aware of what's going on."

"Well, when I was in the house things weren't so bad. But now that I'm not there, I don't know how that poor child is coping. May the Lord just watch over her."

"I promise that when we go back, I will look out for her."

"There's really nothing you can do because Mrs. Baker is a terror and controls that house and everyone in it. She won't give you the chance to approach the child. And besides, what can you do to help and yet you don't live in the house? By day she may pretend, but what happens at night?"

"I'll find a way," Mrs. Dawson promised.

7

WHOEVER LOVES, BELIEVES

Connie opened her eyes and found herself looking up into deep green ones. "You saved my life," she whispered huskily. "I thought I was dreaming all this time but here you are." Her whole body felt like it was on fire and she tried to move around to get some relief.

"Hush," Abel whispered back. "Please don't move around because you were badly injured and the wound on your head and leg might open up again."

"What happened to me?" She struggled to sit up and winced at the pain, tears filling her eyes as she stared helplessly at Abel. She bowed her head, "My mother and Mr. Gerald," the last thing she remembered was being struck and falling.

"Yes, your left leg was broken, but I put it together. You have to be very careful because it hasn't healed fully yet, and we don't want it to break again," but he was really happy to see her awake again. "Are you hungry?"

"I feel like the sky fell on my head," her voice trembled. "I remember everything up until the moment I fell."

"What happened with your parents three days ago?"

"Three days? Is that how long I've been unconscious for?"

"You kept drifting in and out of consciousness and I was so frightened. I thought you would die." Abel shook his head. "All I remember that day is that your parents were shouting so much, and I wanted to come in and help but I'm afraid of Mr. Baker. He is a very harsh man."

"I wish I had died that day," Connie sobbed. "Why didn't I die so that my pain ends?"

"Connie, don't ever say that. I don't want you to die."

"Those people don't want me, and I don't want to live anymore," she looked at him with anger on her face. "Why didn't you just let me die? I told you they were just pretending to be good to me, but they had sinister motives."

"Because you belong with me," he said, and that stunned her for a moment. "Connie, I can't bear to see you continue to suffer like this, but I also don't want you to die. There is always a way out of such trouble."

"There's no way out for me," she shook her head.

Abel had no response for her sad words because he felt equally helpless. The way Mr. and Mrs. Baker had dumped her in the loft to die showed that they were not at all concerned about her wellbeing.

"The important thing for you right now is to get better and then you can think about what to do next," he said instead. Much as he wanted to bring up the issue of them running away together, she was still so young and her parents could create trouble for them. But what if they still thought that she was dead? If she were dead, according to them, then they would never look for her. "Your parents think that you're dead and I overheard them planning on leaving you here and then returning after a few days to bury you out in the forest. They even suggested that the stable should be set on fire so that your body would be burnt."

"That man is not even my father," Connie sniffed, feeling very low. "No wonder he hates me so much."

So much was going on in the Baker household and it seemed like Connie was the victim in so many ways. "Please tell me more."

Connie's face flamed at the shame that rose up within her. What if Abel despised her and believed that she was the one who had asked for trouble? Mr. Baker always told her that she was asking for trouble and he had once told her that she was a temptress. What if Abel thought she was seducing her stepfather or that she herself was the reason for her troubles?

"Connie?" His voice was quiet, but she sensed a hint of anger.

"It's nothing," she mumbled. "I'm tired and I want to sleep now," she turned her head away. She would get better and then run away. There was no way she would ever stay here and continue to be humiliated again.

Abel knew that pressing Connie for more information would get him nowhere. Something sinister was going on in this household but from the way Connie looked, she was not ready to share it all.

Abel knew that men like Mr. Baker were bullies. And as for his wife, she was clearly a woman who had rejected her own offspring, and he couldn't understand it. She loved the other four children, but it seemed like Connie brought out the worst in her. If she could participate in the murder of her own fourteen-year-old daughter, what else would she turn a blind eye to? He had to get Connie away from these people before they completely destroyed her life.

Knowing that Connie didn't trust him enough to share whatever she was going through made him sad. But he would continue looking out for her even if it meant that he would clash with his employers. Connie's safety was important to him. And now that he had discovered that Mr. Baker wasn't her birth father, more than ever, he needed to get her away from here.

∾

"You don't have to ever be afraid of your family again, Connie," Abel whispered as he helped her down the steps from the loft. "I will always be here to protect and help you."

He was quite impressed with her because it was just a few days after the accident, It was a miracle that Mr. Baker had not returned like he'd said he would.

Connie bit her lower lip nervously.

"As soon as I am recovered, I will run away," she murmured as she held onto the railing in the stable and struggled to walk. "If I were stronger, I would leave even today, but I know I would not get far."

"Where will you go?"

She shrugged, "I would like to find my father and ask him why he left me so that my mother and Mr. Baker can torment my life." She refused to let the tears fall, blinking rapidly and willing them away. "I'm so tired of all this anguish."

Abel decided that he would broach the subject of their leaving together now that she had brought it up. "Would you go with me?"

She stopped and looked at him. "Why?"

"Because all I have ever wanted to do for a long time is to protect and also keep you safe, Connie. It hurts me so much when I see you in pain like this."

"Where would we go?"

"What if we went to London? I can find work at the docks and take care of you."

Connie was lost in thought for a brief moment then shook her head. "No. My mother would cause a lot of trouble for you if we get caught. It's better that I leave alone."

"I would never let you go alone, Connie. There are some really bad people out there and they wouldn't hesitate to hurt you badly if you're all alone. Please promise me that you won't try to run away alone."

"But we don't have any money."

"I have some little money I have been saving," Abel told her. "Mr. Blackwell pays me to help around the stable. It's not much, but it will be enough to get us to London and pay for our lodgings for two to three days. Once there, I know I will find work easily since Mr. Randy said workers are always needed at the docks. I'm strong and can work hard."

"But where will we live?"

"Let's deal with one problem at a time," Abel touched her cheek gently and she blushed. "But just promise me that you won't run away alone."

"I promise," she said softly, and he smiled at her so tenderly that she felt butterflies in her stomach.

∽

"According to what my son told me, you and your family are supposed to be on holiday," Joel walked up to the man who was supposed to be his employer but whom he didn't respect at all. "What are you doing back here so soon?"

Mr. Baker looked slightly uncomfortable. He'd intended to sneak back and set the stable on fire, knowing that the horses would escape. But he had to get rid of the body up in the loft before anyone discovered that it was there. He'd been gone for only four days, and as he stepped into the stable, he twitched his nose. But the stable smelled of horse manure and hay as usual. There was no smell of a rotting body, and he sighed in relief. Maybe the quilt they had wrapped the body in was containing the stench.

"Mrs. Baker and I want to renovate the stable and I was coming to find out if one of our neighbours can take the horses for a few days."

"I suppose you've run that by Mr. Blackwell."

"He's not the master of me," Mr. Baker said through clenched teeth.

"He may not be, but he is my direct employer since he is the one who pays my wages, and my instructions from him are that no horses are to be sold or taken out of the estate without his express permission. So, if you want to carry out renovations, don't you think Mr. Blackwell should be made aware of the fact?"

"Your wages are paid by Mr. Malone's estate."

"And Mr. Blackwell is the administrator of the said estate, and as such, he is in charge of all the property that Mr. Malone left. He hasn't informed me of any renovations to be done on the stables, and that means that none of the horses will be moved. In any case, if you want to move the horses, then you should talk to Mr. Blackwell because he has a large stable on his estate and can easily accommodate the fifteen horses."

Seeing that he was defeated, Mr. Baker turned around and left without saying another word. But things weren't so easy for him when he got to Bath where his family was staying in a small, rented cottage just outside the town. It had three rooms, and the four children once again had to share one bedroom, and this annoyed them after being used to the luxury of Malone Manor.

"I want to go home," Mary complained, and her siblings took up the cry.

"Will you be quiet," their mother chased them out of the cottage then turned to their father. "Well? Is the stable burnt to the ground and did you get rid of the body of that girl?"

Mr. Baker shook his head, "Mr. Blackwell as usual is standing in the way."

"I didn't tell you to go and ask for his permission," she said sarcastically.

"I didn't have to, and listen to me, no need to get all snarky with me, woman. Joel is back from Bristol and he wouldn't let me move the horses."

"Who does that man think he is?"

"He is the head stableman, and everything that happens on the estate, and especially to do with the horses, must first be sanctioned by Mr. Blackwell. There was nothing else I could do, so I came back."

"What about that body?" Mrs. Baker wanted to tear her hair out in frustration. "What will happen when someone finds it?"

"Just rest easy," Mr. Baker sighed. "Let's stay here for a few more weeks , during which time someone will have found the body. We will stick to our story that Connie ran away or we thought she did. Let the stablemen deal with the repercussions of that body being found in the loft."

∼

Soon, Connie's hair began to grown back, covering the scar on her head. When she'd asked Abel what he'd done with her hair he'd told her that he was keeping the locks until they got to London and his answer made her content.

"I will take the locks to a wigmaker and have him fashion a nice wig for you. My stepmother says they can do that."

What had surprised them both was when Abel's father and stepmother had returned and come to check on her. They were both so shocked at what had happened that they promised to make sure that she was never harmed again.

"I never knew that your mother was such a wicked woman," Mrs. Dawson told her. "I'll give you some hats to wear and some ointment to put on your head so that the scars will soon fade. And don't worry, your hair will soon grow back again."

"Thank you, Ma'am."

With the help of Abel and his parents who provided for her meals and lodging, the young girl soon regained good health and was stronger. But she knew that all that would soon change because her family couldn't stay away from the manor for too long. She intended to leave as soon as she could. Abel was of the same mind, and it was just a matter of time. Their plan was for her to find work as a maid in one of the homes in London while Abel worked at the docks.

Abel was right; if she ran away alone, she wouldn't be safe. With men like Mr. Baker all over the world, she would never be safe. They had waited hoping that Abel might receive his final wages to add to the money he already had saved up.

"Don't be afraid," Abel murmured. "Remember that no matter how dark the night is, morning comes at last. In but a few days, we'll run away together."

"I'm really scared," she admitted. Abel had told her how her parents had planned on disposing of her body when they thought she was dead. "What if they beat me up again and finally kill me?"

"It won't come to that and remember that I lo…" he cleared his throat. "I care about you so much and will keep you safe. No one will ever harm you again. My parents also know what happened and promised that they will help you. You don't have to be afraid again."

"Thank you," Connie smiled. Like Abel, she hadn't liked Mrs. Dawson at first, but in this past days the woman had proved to be a good person. Connie was happy that Abel was getting on much better with his stepmother, and his father was happier. He was making plans on getting them out of Ritter's Village and she would be patient.

∽

Connie decided to brave one final return to her childhood prison to gather a few things she could call her own. She especially wanted to take her doll. Even though she was now almost a woman, the doll spoke of love to her and she did not want to leave even one slice of her heart in this evil place.

Knowing her parents and siblings were away made the prospect of stepping inside the house far less frightening.

Making her way upstairs Connie smiled. Her heart felt free at the prospect of finally being far away from her abusers, somewhere they would never find her.

With her doll, and a handful of other items in her bag, Connie almost skipped downstairs, but it was her heart that would skip next. She heard the voices of her siblings outside. Her family had returned earlier than expected. Running down the stairs toward the kitchen and out to freedom Connie failed to see the shadow behind the back door.

She threw the door open, ready to run, and standing before her was her mother.

Mrs. Baker's face went white, as if staring at a ghost. She gathered her composure and stuttered awkwardkly.

"T-t-there you are," Connie didn't dare look into her mother's face for fear of what she would see there. This was the woman who had brought her into the world and then tried to take her life. Connie wanted to ask her mother why she hated her so much.

Then she heard her siblings' voices as they came running to the backyard. They stopped short when they saw her, noticing the crutches under her arm.

. . .

"Look who it is, the runaway! Running away from home like a vagabond, and now look at you! What happened to your le, silly girl? Were you eating from the dustbins? And why did you decide to come back when before you felt that you could live without us?"

"Just see how spiky her hair is," Anne stuck her tongue out at Connie. "You are still so ugly, and I can't bear to look at your unpleasant face."

"Leave her alone," Mrs. Baker said and gave Connie a look she couldn't decipher. "Get into the house. Grant, find John; then you can go and help your father bring our luggage into the house."

Connie brushed the tears away as she struggled to think what to do next, when John came running out.

"Did someone hurt you?" He asked in his small voice and she looked at him. He looked genuinely troubled at her plight, and she wondered what was going on with him.

"John!" Their mother's voice was impatient, but the small boy didn't move.

"Connie, I'm sorry that you're hurting." He then rose to his feet and rushed into the house, leaving her staring after him. What had just happened?

"Here," Abel appeared as if from nowhere and held out a hand to help her. He had followed her to the house, concerned that she was taking some time to return. "Connie, don't worry. We will still get you away from here. Play as if you remember nothing, and soon we will find a way for you to flee."

Then he noticed her staring at the kitchen door.

"John," she said, shaking her head. "I don't understand why he just stopped to speak to me when he and the others have been nothing but mean to me all the time. And he even said he was sorry that I got hurt."

"Let me help you to your feet. It's so sad that even after being away from you they are still so mean."

"I hate them so much," Connie started crying. "Why didn't they just stay away forever?"

"Connie, you're just too gentle and kind-hearted to carry hate in your heart. Don't worry, just work on getting better so we can leave this place."

"Connie," her mother called out. "Get in here at once."

Abel raised her to her feet and then handed her the crutch. "Remember to keep silent no matter how much you're insulted. Morning will soon come, Connie; just hold onto your faith. Things will get better, I promise."

She nodded and hobbled to the kitchen, bracing herself for a blow, surprised when none landed on her.

"What did you do while we were gone?" Dinah Baker couldn't look at her daughter for the mixed feelings she had in her heart. Guilt was foremost but she pushed it down.

"Nothing, mother, I found myself in the stables but don't remember how I got there. I must have fallen because my head hurt and my leg was in an awful way. I have no memory of how I got in such a state." Connie whispered. She hated to lie, but did not want her captors to suspect she remembered their cruelty.

"We thought you had run away! Who took care of you?"

"Nobody, Mother. I did my best to fix my leg with what I found beside me and did what I could to look after myself. I cried out but no one answered. Because I looked such an awful state I hid from anyone who came to the house." The last thing she wanted was to get Abel or his parents in trouble. "I learned how to crawl, so I was able to take care of myself. I tilled the garden so there are vegetables," she said, knowing that she wouldn't even be thanked for that. Well, Abel had actually done nearly all the work, but she wasn't about to let her mother find out how much time she had spent with Abel.

"What about that imbecile, Joel Pierson's son? Did he run away or just get drunk like the other louts?" Her mother twisted her lips. "If the estate wasn't paying them, I would have gotten rid of them ages ago. But that Blackwell fellow won't even listen when I tell him that these workers are all disrespectful."

"I didn't see anyone, but the horses were tended to, so I guess the stablemen were around."

Her mother grunted, "Prepare lunch for us. We're tired after our long journey."

"Yes Mother."

Connie had just started peeling potatoes for lunch when John entered the kitchen once again. She ignored him because she wasn't sure what he wanted.

"Can I help you?" He came to stand next to her. "Then we could peel them faster."

"No," she quickly shook her head. "If Mama finds you here, she will whip me. Please just go and play outside, John. I will soon be finished."

The boy stood there for a while and then twisted his lips. "Connie, I was mean to you before and I'm sorry."

She stopped what she was doing and just stared at her brother. Who was this little boy, and where was her usually rough and unkind brother? He and Grant had always played pranks on her, then laughed at her discomfiture and humiliation.

"Please, I just want to be your friend."

"Just go, John, I hear someone coming and I don't want to get into trouble."

"Yes," then he did a surprising thing and kissed her cheek before running out of the kitchen just as her mother walked into the kitchen.

"What did John want?" She asked Connie roughly, worried Connie may have said something incriminating.

"I think he's hungry and I told him lunch will soon be ready," she finished peeling the potatoes and then carried them to the large sink. She could feel her mother's eyes on her but refused to feel intimidated even though she kept expecting a blow to land on her back. It surprised her that for the next one hour her mother just sat in the kitchen watching her as she prepared their lunch. Once she had served the food into bowls, she waited for her mother to leave so she could carry it to the dining room.

"I'll get the others," Mrs. Baker said, and Connie sighed with relief. She couldn't understand what her mother was doing but she would be silent and keep her head down.

～

"How did that girl survive the time that we were away," Mr. Baker asked his wife. "How is it that she isn't dead?"

"That is something I'd really like to find out for myself. Connie must have had some help from people around her, but she told me she was here alone, well, apart from the stablemen."

"We have to be careful that no one finds out what happened or that she didn't tell anyone about her injuries. These people who work on the estate are such loud mouths and I wouldn't put it past any of them not to tell Mr. Blackwell. That girl will always be trouble for us, and we need to think about what to do with her."

"Let's be quiet for a while until we know what is going on. She must have told someone, and I don't want Blackwell descending on us."

8
NIGHT OF TERROR

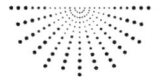

T*wo Weeks Later*

"No matter how long the darkness lasts, morning will soon come," Connie muttered to herself as she swept the kitchen. Once again, Mary and Anne had caused a mess, but this time she hadn't said a word. Still they called out to their mother who came to the kitchen and Connie knew what was coming next. But to her surprise and that of her siblings, her mother didn't hit her like she was wont to do. She just glared at her and told her to clean up the mess and then left the kitchen.

It had been a strange two weeks since they returned from their holiday. Not once had anyone hit her but she heard the snide remarks made by her siblings, apart from John. And though her mother still shouted at her, she hadn't once hit her, nor had Mr. Baker.

Even as she swept, she could see her sisters watching her. They soon got tired of insulting her and left. Her leg was throbbing and more than anything, she really wanted to sit down. But if she took a moment to rest and her mother or siblings came by, there would be more trouble.

A door slammed somewhere upstairs, startling her. Probably her sisters or brothers fighting, and she shrugged, returning to what she was doing. Then she heard two heavy sets of footsteps as if someone was chasing the other. That was definitely not her siblings and she became alert.

"Leave me alone, Gerald, I've had enough of your lies and infidelities."

"Don't talk to me as if I'm one of your children," Gerald growled. "You are my wife and I have a right to demand for you to do whatever I want. Come back before I get really angry."

"That will never happen, and you can just go right back to the brothel from whence you came. Find someone who is desperate enough to put up with your unfaithfulness all the time. I warned you the last time you were unfaithful that I wouldn't stand for it. What kind of a man are you who cannot keep his hands to himself?"

"How far do you think you can push me? How long will you continue denying me my husbandly rights?"

"You brought this upon yourself when you decided that you would give your favours to every woman in Ritter's Village; the good the bad and the ugly. I don't even know why I bother putting up with you and yet you'll never change."

"Come back here, woman!" Gerald roared.

"No, and I suggest you get out of this house before I really get upset. Get away and stay away from me until you learn how to be a good husband," her mother was shouting.

"Come back here, Dinah." When she heard the footsteps drawing closer to the kitchen, she knew that trouble was coming her way.

Connie dropped the long broom and hobbled out of the kitchen, racing toward the stable where she knew she would be safe. Her heart was pounding as she painfully climbed the steps to the loft.

Once she got in, she bolted the door and sat down on the narrow cot that Abel had found from somewhere. She was shivering but not with the cold. It seemed like her mother and stepfather fought so much these days and then one or both of them would find the excuse of hurling insults at her. But at least the beatings had ceased, except that the insults had more than doubled.

She heard someone coming up the steps and thinking that it was Abel she walked to the door and drew the bolt back. He must have returned from running errands for her stepfather and seen her fleeing from the kitchen and come to check up on her. She smiled as she thought about the young man who always looked out for her.

"I…" the words died on her lips when she saw who it was. Her stepfather entered the loft, looking around with interest and she stumbled backward. Then he turned his eyes on her and the expression in them terrified her. She knew that she was in a lot of trouble. It was clear that Abel wasn't back yet. Why hadn't she asked who it was before opening the door as Abel had warned her to always do?

"Nice, cosy place you have here," Mr. Baker licked his lips.

"Please leave me alone," her voice trembled. "Please."

She appealed to his humanity, but he merely growled at her.

He snarled as Connie shook her head and lifted her arms to push him away. "You know what girls like you deserve, don't you? And just to remind you, I'm not your father. To me you're just another foolish woman."

Connie sobbed weakly.

∼

Abel didn't like being away from the estate because he was very protective of Connie. But after running around the village market in search of apples and apricots which he was laughingly informed weren't in season, he realised that Mr. Baker had sent him on a fools' errand. Abel suspected that the errand was clearly just a ploy for him to be away from the stables so he could have access to Connie.

As long as Abel was working in the stables, the man never set foot in there. And even when he did, it was just to bark out unnecessary orders to Abel and the other stablemen. Randy and Nick always ignored his instructions, laughing behind his back and mocking him. Abel's father was now in charge of the dairy animals and so rarely came to the stable.

"I have been deceived," he muttered as he started running back to the estate. He was very careful not to let anyone in the manor see him slip into the stable and was just in time to see Mr. Baker starting up the steps as he glanced furtively around to make sure no one was around. This boded ill for Connie because Abel had noticed how the man looked at the poor girl.

Abel slipped into the stall closest to the entrance of the stable, quieting the nervous horse. The others neighed softly, and the young man prayed that they wouldn't begin stamping on the floor. He wanted to know what Mr. Baker was really up to.

As Abel watched from the shadows, Mr. Baker climbed the steps up to the loft. He'd told Connie to always bolt the door from the inside and never open it unless for him. He wanted to shout for her not to open the door but when he heard her drawing the bolt back, he knew it was too late.

Creeping from his hiding place he carefully climbed up the steps.

"If you scream, I'll strangle you," Abel stepped into the loft to find that Mr. Baker was struggling to with his hands pressed to Connie's throat to prevent her from screaming.

Abel let out a shout as he rushed towards the man who had been so bent on carrying out his heinous act that he hadn't been aware of his surroundings.

"What…" Mr. Baker looked shocked as he dropped Connie who fell to her knees rubbing her neck and gasping for air.

Abel didn't allow the man to say a word but socked him hard in the jaw.

"What kind of a shameless man are you," the young man was swifter on his feet and the blow that Mr. Baker threw in retaliation flew into the air harmlessly. "She is only a child, your child and yet you want to hurt her," he would never forget the picture of how terrified Connie had looked when he'd burst into the loft.

"She is not my daughter," Mr. Baker whimpered as he raised his hands to ward off more blows that came at him from all sides. Abel was so enraged that he wasn't thinking straight. He wanted to hurt this man for his cruel treatments over the years. He was an aspiring pugilist and was swift on his feet, unlike Mr. Baker whose overindulgences in the finer things of life had rendered him heavy and slow.

"She is only a child," Abel lashed out and pushed the man out of the loft. "And you can be sure that I will let the whole world know that a seemingly respectable man like you would lust after a child, your own child."

"No," Mr. Baker was now really scared, and his face was bruised. He tried to run from more blows even as Abel lashed out one last time. Mr. Baker ducked, missed a step and went tumbling down the steps even as Connie screamed then quickly covered her mouth.

"I didn't push him," Abel paled when he saw the man lying very still at the bottom of the steps, two of which had broken as he fell. "Connie, I didn't push him. He was ducking and stumbled," he said. "Put on another dress, we're getting out of here right now."

Connie's hands were trembling, and she could barely dress herself, but she managed, grabbing an old shawl and covering herself with it. Abel went down first, helping Connie over the broken steps and then they both stood over the unconscious man just as Mrs. Baker and her children burst into the barn. It was obvious that Connie's scream had carried to the house.

"What did you do," Mrs. Baker screamed at them. "You have killed my husband."

"No Ma'am," Abel saw Randy and Nick entering the stable. He tried to push Connie out of her mother's line of sight but Mrs. Baker saw her.

"You evil child," she screamed then turned to Mary. "Take a horse and run to the village and bring the constable down here. These criminals have killed your father. Tell him to hurry up and get here before they escape."

Abel wanted to run away from the trouble he knew was sure to follow but he could never leave Connie. If it meant dying for her, he was prepared to do so.

Mrs. Baker turned to the other two stablemen who had also run into the stable. "Don't just stand there like imbeciles. Restrain this mad man and don't let him out of your sight. He is a murderer and has killed my husband." Randy and Nick jumped on Abel, mindful of his bloody fists. "Mary has gone to bring the constable so these two can be arrested."

Connie watched helplessly as Abel was dragged away by the two men.

~

Abel hung his head, not speaking a word. "Son, don't you have anything to say in your own defence?"

He had been dragged away by the two stablemen who had tied him up with ropes until the constable came to take him away. When his father had followed down to the village precinct, he'd told Abel that they were doing all they could to get him freed. That was three days ago, during which he'd prayed that Connie would be safe. His father and Mrs. Dawson had visited him just this morning before he was arraigned before the village magistrate. But it turned out that the magistrate was away in London, and a judge was standing in for him since Mrs. Baker was demanding justice for her husband.

Justice Maurice Lamb was on a sabbatical from his London duties and had agreed to try the case in his colleague's absence.

"Mr. Abel, why did you push Mr. Baker? Do you know that the man is now paralysed and cannot walk again? This is a very serious crime and one that could have you facing prison for a very long time."

The small courtroom was not full because the judge had decided to keep the public out, much to Mrs. Baker's chagrin. She was a woman who liked everything to be as public and dramatic as possible, especially when she claimed to be the injured party. The only people present were Mrs. Baker and her two daughters Mary and Anne, and Abel's parents apart from the court officials and the two village constables.

"I didn't push Mr. Baker. He fell as he was trying to get away when I confronted him about attacking Connie in the loft."

"Liar," Mrs. Baker screamed, and the judge gave her a look that silenced her.

"What do you mean he attacked Miss Baker? According to the charge made by Mrs. Baker, this girl called Connie enticed Mr. Baker to her room and then you attacked him. According to her, this attack was planned by the two of you."

Abel looked up at Justice Lamb, knowing that his life was over anyway. But he would make a plea on behalf of Connie for he saw something like compassion in the judge's eyes.

"This girl you speak of is just fourteen years old, your honour. And she is Mr. Baker's stepdaughter. When I got to the loft, Mr. Baker had her pinned to the wall, strangling her so she couldn't scream. Your honour, Constance is only fourteen years old."

"Mmh!" The judge rubbed his chin thoughtfully. "It doesn't say that in this report that I have here," his eyes turned to Mrs. Baker. "This girl is your daughter, isn't she?"

"Yes."

"And where is the said girl?"

"She ran away after all the trouble she caused," Mrs. Baker hissed. "No one has seen her since."

From the look the judge gave her it was obvious that he didn't believe her, and neither did Abel.

"I will hold this prisoner pending the constables finding the missing girl," Justice Lamb said. "Once she is found and brought here, the case shall continue. Have it in mind that she's been missing for three days and could be anywhere."

"Well," Mrs. Baker said almost haughtily, and Abel feared for Connie like never before. This was a woman capable of doing anything, just so she would look like she was on the right side of the law. "It would be a waste of time because that girl will never be found. She is too cunning and has made good her escape."

∼

John Baker stood in the shadows of Mr. Pitcher's house and listened to his mother speaking to the old gentleman. He couldn't hear what they were saying but he was troubled. He'd seen his mother bring in some people he didn't recognize, and they had carried Connie to this man's house.

In the past, he had insulted his sister but ever since they had gone to Bath, something within him had changed. It had happened one night when his parents were talking and thought that the four of them were sleeping. That was when he found out that his sister was dead, and his parents had something to do with it. Too shocked to speak he had crept back to bed and spent the night thinking about Connie.

She was kind and never fought with anyone, but they had always been so mean to her. There and then the small boy repented of his horrible actions toward Connie. So when they returned home and he saw that she was alive, his joy knew no bounds. And from then on, he watched over her just to see that she was all right. On the day his father had fallen from the loft, he had watched in silence as Abel was dragged way and then bound with ropes so the constable could come and arrest him. And once Randy and Nick had taken Abel away, his mother had turned on Connie, kicked her so hard on her injured leg that John was sure he'd heard it snap. When she fell on the floor screaming in pain, his mother had picked up a piece of wood and beaten her so badly that she became unconscious. He couldn't bear to see Connie being hurt and he'd flung himself over her body. That was what had stopped his mother from hitting her anymore.

He had tried to rouse Connie so she could run away from more harm, but then his mother had returned with two men, strangers he'd never seen before, and they had put Connie on an old ox cart. John had followed them on foot, running all the way until they had arrived at this house. That was three days ago, and he had been coming here ever since just to make sure Connie was all right. So far, he hadn't seen any sign of her, but his mother was inside speaking to the old man who had come home a few minutes ago.

John felt helpless because he didn't know who to tell what had happened. Abel had been taken away and he had no idea where he was.

9

DAMSEL IN DISTRESS

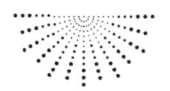

This wasn't the loft, Connie thought as she opened her eyes and realized that she was lying on a narrow bed. The room was large but bare, and its walls were painted with a dark colour so that the sunlight didn't even brighten it.

"I see that you're now awake, Princess," she heard the rough voice and her eyes quickly turned toward the door from whence it had come. Then horror filled her heart as she recognized the man standing in the doorway. "I'm sorry I wasn't here three days ago to receive you, but I see that your mother did the right thing and brought you to me as I demanded." Connie was shocked at his words. Connie wasn't surprised that her mother had brought her into this man's house after beating her until she became unconscious. Henry Pitcher was a man she detested and feared in equal measure. He was her stepfather's friend and together, the two men had caused her a lot of trouble over the past few months. The man would find any excuse to come by the house and the way he looked at her had frightened her. Once he'd even tried to grab her, but Abel suddenly appeared, and he'd quickly left. Now she was here in this room with him and she wanted to scream, but her throat felt clogged.

"What am I doing here?" She sat up slowly, her whole body aching. Had he attacked her while she was unconscious and robbed her of her virtue? She realised that apart from the bruises on her arms and legs, her virtue was intact, and she sent a thankful prayer heavenwards. Wait, the man had said she'd been brought here three days ago. "Who brought me here?"

Mr. Pitcher only giggled, and Connie realized that he was totally inebriated. She was weak after the beating her mother had meted out once Abel had been dragged away. He was probably dead, and it was all her fault.

"Will my pain ever end," she murmured, momentarily forgetting about the man who was swaying drunkenly in the doorway.

"Did you say…" he hiccupped and giggled again, and she noticed that he was carrying a bottle of whisky under his arm. It was nearly all gone. "You," he wagged a finger at her. "My wife…"

"What?" She paled and would have swooned but forced herself to remain alert. If she lost consciousness again there's no telling what this man would do to her.

Instead of looking at him, her eyes darted around the room as if searching for something, a weapon with which to protect herself. It was a large room, yes, but drab, and the thick carpet on the floor must have once been beautiful. But it was now full of holes as if it had been eaten by rats. The curtains looked old and worn out, and the only weapon she could see was the small poker by the fireplace. She looked at it and then at Mr. Pitcher, wondering if she could get to it in time. This time she was going to fight for her life because she was tired of always being the victim.

Connie couldn't believe that this was a room in Henry Pitcher's house. Whenever the man would come to the manor, all he did was brag about how wealthy he was. He would compare everything in the manor to what he had in his own house. But this looked like a neglected house or maybe the other rooms were better than this. Still, that wasn't her problem right now, getting as far away from him as possible was. She felt her leg, thankful that it hadn't been broken again when her mother kicked her.

"I paid money for you, so you are mine," Connie turned her eyes back to her jailor. He pulled away from the door and stumbled toward her. She scrambled off the bed and darted toward the window. Even though the room was on the first floor, she was ready to jump to get away from this man.

"My wife," he giggled again and moved forward. He wasn't looking where he was going, and his foot got caught in one of the holes in the carpet. As he tried to pull his leg out, he stumbled and the bottle flew out of his hands, struck one of the walls, broke and splattered its scarce contents all over the wall, floor and old carpet. The smell of cheap gin immediately permeated the room. But Connie didn't care about that, she watched as the man flailed his hands and stumbled backwards.

She heard a sickening thump as he hit the mantle of the small fireplace hard. Then he crumpled to the floor like an empty sack and lay still.

Connie stood by the window in shock for a long while, too scared to approach the man on the floor just in case he was pretending to be unconscious. But when nearly an hour had passed without him moving, she realized that he wasn't pretending.

So she moved forward carefully but was also careful to stay at a safe distance from him. It was the trail of blood that caused her to scream. A few minutes later she heard footsteps running up the stairs.

The door was pushed open, and two men stepped into the room. She didn't recognize them but that didn't matter right now.

"He fell," she said needlessly as the men looked around and took in the broken bottle and wrinkled their noses at the smell of gin.

"I have warned him time and time again about his drinking," one of the men said. "And who are you?"

"The new maid," Connie said for lack of anything else to say.

The answer apparently satisfied both men for they immediately ignored her and knelt down beside the still unconscious man. "Mr. Pitcher," one of them shook him.

"Is he... dead?" Connie was trembling. This was the second man in just days who had tried to attack her then fallen and gotten badly hurt. Seeing Mr. Pitcher lying so still on the floor reminded her of her stepfather, and she realised that she had no idea how he was doing. Had he died? And what would happen to Abel, if he hadn't already been lynched?

Once the men had carried Mr. Pitcher out of her room, Connie sat down on the bed and covered her face with her hands. She should run away but where would she go? She had no money and was also very weak. The door opened slowly, and she quickly looked up, expecting to see one or both men returning.

"John, what are you doing here?"

Her brother shrugged as he closed the door and then turned the key. "Are you all right?"

"John, how did you get into this house? Where is Mama?"

"I saw Mama beating you but I'm too little to help, so I threw myself on you and then she had to stop hitting you. I tried to wake you up so you could run away," he was weeping silently. "But then she called those men to carry you away, and I followed them here and was hiding in the shrubs behind the house. I have been coming to see you every day, but there was no one at the house at first. Then the old man came, and I saw Mama talking to him, and when she left, I heard you screaming."

"Mama will be looking for you. You should go home."

"Connie, can I stay here with you?"

"This is not our house and Mama will be looking for you."

"But I want to stay here with you."

"Come here," she told him, and he approached her. "John, I know you want to stay here with me, but Mama will be worried."

"Connie, I don't like Mama anymore."

She smiled sadly, "Don't say that, because it's not right."

"But Mama beat you up and I couldn't help you."

"You're still a small boy and I don't want you to get hurt. Go back home, but you can come and see me at any time."

"I saw that man, Papa's friend. He is sleeping in the other room."

"Did you see anyone else?"

John shook his head. "When you screamed, I followed those two men who carried the old man to the other room. Is he dead?"

"I don't know," she whispered. "He fell and hit his head."

"Like Papa?" He looked scared but she saw something like relief in his eyes.

"How is Papa?"

"The doctor came and said that he cannot walk. Mary and Anne were crying, but I left them there because I followed Mama and those men when they brought you here."

"John, you have to go back home."

"Will you be coming home again?"

Connie shook her head, "I can't ever come home again, John. I have to stay here for a few days and then I will come."

He looked like he didn't believe her, but he shrugged, then walked across the room and picked up something from the floor. "Is this your money?"

"Let me see," she held out her hand and he dropped three farthings into her palm. "Thank you."

"Can I come and see you again?"

"Yes, but you have to be very careful, because I don't want you to get into trouble."

∼

Constantinople wasn't what Abel expected but he didn't have time to gape at the magnificent oriental buildings. According to what Captain Trent Lamb had told him, they were on their way to join the rest of the British fleet that was set to sail to the north shore of the Black Sea. The aim of the allied troops was to lay siege to the Russian fortress of Sevastopol.

"Stay by my side always," Captain Trent told him. "We may make a naval soldier of you yet."

Though being a soldier was the last thing Abel had ever thought of becoming, he knew that he owed his life to his master. Instead of tossing him in prison as Mrs. Baker had been insisting, Justice Lamb had spoken with his son and they decided that Abel would be his valet and follow him to the battlefield. The Crimean War was raging, and Captain Trent had been called in to head up one of the newer units, hence their presence in the Peninsula.

Abel's only regret was not knowing what had happened to Connie. The judge had insisted on Connie being brought to the court room and even sent two village constables to the Malone Estate to search for her. But Connie was really gone, and Abel was fearful that she might be dead. Mrs. Dinah had looked smug when the judge had announced that the case would go on without her presence. But she was soon fuming when instead of being thrown into prison like she'd wanted, the judge said he would deal with Abel personally.

"You look distracted," Captain Trent commented as they travelled toward the small coastal town of Agura to meet up with the rest of their troops and then board the warships that would take them to Sevastopol. "Are you still thinking about what happened?"

"Not really," Abel said.

"Is it about that young girl who went missing?"

"Yes."

"Why?"

"There's something that just didn't ring true about Connie running away. She wasn't well enough to run very far."

"So what are you saying?"

"I have a strong feeling that Mrs. Baker did something to Connie." And Abel went ahead to tell Captain Trent all about how Connie's parents had broken her leg and their plans to get rid of the body when they thought she was dead. "I have a feeling that Connie is in a lot of trouble," he finished.

"You should have told my father all that."

Abel shrugged, "I tried to speak up, but Mrs. Baker was shouting too much and causing a lot of ruckus. She is a very nasty woman, and I really fear for Connie's life."

"Well, like my Mama says, if you can't do anything about it, you can pray. You're here and Connie is wherever she is. Instead of worrying about her why don't you pray?"

"Thank you, Captain," Abel felt some relief about the issue that was bothering him. His Mama had taught him to pray, and he realized that ever since she had died years ago, he'd stopped praying. It was time for him to renew his relationship to the Saviour his mother had introduced him to when he was still a small boy, the One who listened to and answered prayers.

~

Summer 1855 – Ritter's Village, Cambridge

"You're a worthless woman," Tabitha Pitcher hissed at Connie. "You can't even follow simple instructions."

Connie bowed her head and didn't say a word back. She couldn't believe that she had been in this household for close to two years now. After Henry's unfortunate accident, his sisters had come to live in his house claiming that they were there to take care of their brother. In actual fact they were only there because Henry was a rich man and they wanted to make sure that if he died they would get his property.

Even though life was terrible, and she wanted to run away many times, Connie felt a little safer in this household because her supposed husband was bedridden and couldn't hurt her, at least not physically. But the man never stopped insulting her as did his sisters.

"Did you know that your foolish friend is back from the war in Europe? And he is now engaged to a beautiful woman called Catherine Landon and she is Justice Lamb's niece." The two sisters laughed at Connie, but she refused to let them get to her. She was just glad to find out that Abel hadn't died as John had told her. For the past two years her little brother had become a common visitor to the house and always brought her news of what was happening back at the manor. It was he who had told her that Abel had died in prison, according to their mother and she was now happy to hear that he was still alive. But the news that he was now engaged to another woman hurt her deeply. Yet she wouldn't give the Pitcher sisters the satisfaction of knowing that their words hurt her.

"You will always be a useless woman no one wants."

"Mercy, we don't have to keep standing here and talking to this deaf and dumb woman. We have things to do," Tabitha picked up her parasol and small purse. "Make sure you bring afternoon tea to Henry. We can't have you starving our brother." And with their noses in the air, the two women left the house.

Henry was staring at the ceiling when Connie entered his bedchamber. "I have brought you some tea," she said. Even though the man was paralysed from the neck down, Connie was always afraid of entering his bedchamber alone. She kept expecting him to jump out of bed and attack her and she was always so wary.

"Leave me alone," he mumbled.

"Miss Tabitha said I should bring you your tea."

"Are you deaf?" He shouted and she flinched. "What kind of a worthless woman did I get the misfortune to land myself with?"

Connie felt that the attack was unwarranted. "I didn't ask to be brought to your house, Sir, and I'm only doing my best to see that you are comfortable."

"I bet you're wishing I was dead so you could claim my wealth as my widow."

"I'm here as a servant and not as anything else. Whatever you and my mother had planned was done without my consent and so I am merely your maid."

He gave her a look that frightened her, and she was just glad that he was a complete invalid and couldn't get up to hurt her.

"Would you like me to give you your tea now?"

"Just go away, you wicked woman," he hissed, baring his teeth and reminding her of a wolf that she'd once seen at the Malone estate.

"Very well then," she twisted her lips knowing that the ungrateful man would tell his sisters that she had refused to give him his tea.

10
BROKEN PROMISES

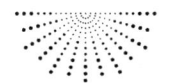

Few Days Before

Abel was glad when he spied the shores of England. He was worried that his master might be dying after the terrible injuries he'd suffered. Captain Trent was a strategist and had tried to advise his naval colleagues of some ill moves they were making, but his voice was overridden. As a result, their ship had been hit by one of the Russian Warships, and as Captain Trent went to the aid of his wounded officers, he was also wounded.

Abel had sent a telegram to Justice Lamb who had organised for them to return home. That was when Abel appreciated the fact that powerful people could do anything. Money was everything in this world as he'd learnt on the battlefield. While Captain Trent was very good at what he did, he was still spared the worst of the battle. Their ship was not really a man of war but more like a supplies ship. They had been attacked by the Russian ship probably for the supplies they carried but mercifully the other British ships had quickly come to their aid. Still, Captain Trent was crushed beneath one of the large iron masts and his legs and hands were pinned down. The army doctor had said all his limbs might have to be amputated but Abel had refused to allow it to happen, instead sending an urgent telegram to the judge, who made all the arrangements for them to return to England. Abel felt sad about the other soldiers they had left back in the fields under deplorable conditions. But still, he was glad to be home.

In the one-and-a-half years he'd been at Captain Trent's side in war, Abel had seen the terrible conditions that the injured soldiers were in. Many of them died, not because of the injuries they had received from the enemy, but because of unhygienic conditions in the medical tents. Getting Captain Trent away from that had been his priority.

The moment Abel and Captain Trent got home, the latter's mother fussed over him, and it made Abel miss his own mother all the more. He knew that he didn't have any reason to feel jealous of his master, but he just couldn't help it. It would be nice to know that when he got home from the war that there would be someone waiting for him. And when he was over there in the thick of the war, there would be a person back at home praying for him.

"I'm just happy that it wasn't as bad as I feared," Mrs. Lamb wiped her son's brow and Captain Trent, all twenty-seven-year-old muscled man that he was, grinned at Abel.

"It feels good to be home, Mama."

"Which reminds me, your cousin is coming down for a few days," Mrs. Lamb's mouth tightened, and Abel wondered why she would be unhappy at her niece's visit.

"Not Catherine," Trent scowled.

Mrs. Lamb nodded, "Yes, your cousin Catherine. Her mother sent me a letter to say that she was feeling down in the dumps because her engagement fell through. The man changed his mind and decided to marry someone else, and Catherine is devastated. Margaret thought a few days out here in the country would do her some good."

"Mama, do you really think that's a good idea? Cousin Kate is trouble enough without her having a broken heart. What happens when she comes here and is all moody and whinny? We shouldn't have to put up with all that, Ma. If my sisters Rebecca and Grace were here, then it would be all right, for then they could giggle with her and make her happy. But it's only me at home now, so what is Cousin Kate supposed to do around here?" He looked down at himself, "And as you can see, I'm an invalid and can't be expected to wait on her day and night or even entertain her. Mama, you need to send a telegram to Cousin Kate and tell her not to come, at least not for another few months."

His mother merely shrugged, "You'll have to find something to do to keep your cousin entertained for the few days that she will be here. Who knows, she might even help nurse you back to health."

"Mama please, I would rather be in the middle of the battle out in the Crimean Peninsula than have to face a weepy and broody Cousin Kate. And as for her being my nurse, Mama, I have Abel here, and it's better that way."

"Please do this for me, Trent. It will only be for a few days and then she will go back home and face the world."

Trent turned to Abel, "At least say that you'll be here with me."

"I will, Sir," Abel said, getting more curious about this Catherine girl.

"Thank you. I know that you want to visit your folks, but I don't think there's anything you'll be doing there. You no longer work on Malone Estate, and we want to avoid that nasty woman who wanted you thrown in prison, so this is the best place for you to be until I'm well enough to return to Europe. And besides, I need you to help me with some correspondence. I may be out of the war, but my men still need me, and it is also good to keep them encouraged."

"Yes Sir. But would it be all right if I went to visit my folks just for a day or two?"

"You may, as long as you don't go getting into any kind of trouble, Abel. We've been away for two years, and it would be prudent to put the past to rest and move on. Don't go stirring up trouble where there's none."

"I'll stay out of trouble," Abel said, knowing full well that he wasn't going to keep his promise. He had missed Connie and longed to find out if she had ever returned. Somehow, he didn't believe that she had run away as her mother had said. No, something else had happened to Connie. He would ask his parents if in the two years that he'd been away, they'd heard anything about Connie.

"Not a word," his stepmother told him later that evening when they were relaxing before the small fire after a sumptuous dinner that she'd prepared. He could see that a lot of things had changed since he'd last been home, and his parents looked so much happier. "We have tried asking about Connie, but the family is tight lipped about any information to do with her, so we believe that she did actually run away."

"I just hope that she is all right," he said. Then he remembered something, "What about Mr. Blackwell? Do you think he might know something about Connie?"

"Why would he when he never really had anything to do with her? Besides, Mr. Blackwell suffered a stroke about the same time that Connie went missing and it's now his son Mark who runs the estate, and I doubt that he has ever heard of Connie. The young girl ran away and there's nothing anyone can do about it, least of all you, Abel. I don't want you to go and confront Mrs. Baker in any way so please stay out of trouble."

"I promise that I won't cause any trouble," he said resignedly. Perhaps he should just forget about Connie and presume her dead. But something deep within refused to let go, only he didn't want to agitate his father. "What has been happening in Ritter's Village," he said instead.

"Tell us about your time in Europe," his father cut in when he saw his sad face. "The few times that I've happened to run into the good judge when he's down here from London, the man has only had good things to say about you."

Abel smiled. "He saved my life when I thought all was lost. Pa, what happened to Mr. Baker?"

"The man is still paralyzed and can't walk. He rarely leaves the house, and it is his wife who now runs things, if I can call it that. Of course, even though he's bedridden, Mr. Blackwell is still in charge overall. What I can say is that the Bakers are having a hard time since Constance disappeared. It's like the neighbours have all turned against them and they've been shunned and keep to themselves."

"And so they should be," Abel said with tight lips. "They made her life hell and I hope they never know peace in their lives again."

"Abel, don't be so bitter," his father warned in a mild tone. "People's lives are their own business and it won't do to get angry at them. What are you plans now that you're back from the war?"

"Captain Trent has asked me to go back to his parents' house and help him with correspondence and running other errands. At least the doctor said he wouldn't lose his limbs, but he's still very weak and I have to attend to him as his valet."

"That's a good thing because it wouldn't do for you to remain idle. You've grown up and matured in just two years and I'm so happy about that. If you do well, I'm sure the good captain will recommend you for something bigger and better."

Abel stayed two days with his family, and he was sad to leave them, seeing how close they had become. "Thank you for taking such good care of my father," he told Mrs. Dawson as he hugged her. "I know I wasn't the easiest child to put up with, but thank you for overlooking all my childish tantrums."

Anita Dawson had tears in her eyes as she hugged her stepson. More than anything in the world she had wanted this young man's acceptance into this family. "And I'm sorry that I wasn't the mother you needed, but now I have changed and want only good for you. Will you please forgive me?"

Abel nodded glad to note that he really meant it, and this was the chance to start all over again with his family. "And if it's all right with you, may I please call you Ma?"

"I would like that very much," she said, letting the tears fall. "I'll always be your mother and I pray that things will work out for you. Please come and see us before you leave for London."

"I promise to do that."

He walked away with a much lighter heart knowing that he had made peace with his stepmother at last. He had just slipped out of the gate when he thought he heard someone running behind him. So he stopped and turned, surprised to find a young boy running towards him. Recognizing him as the Bakers' youngest son John, he folded his arms across his chest and waited to hear what the boy had to say.

"Mr. Abel," John was panting when he reached him. "I saw you yesterday and wanted to come and speak with you, but Mama didn't let me out of the house. We've all had the chicken pox, and she keeps us indoors."

"I'm surprised to see you running after me, John; in the past, all you did was hurl insults at me."

The twelve-year-old looked down and Abel was surprised to see shame on his face. "I'm sorry," he mumbled. "I wasn't a nice person before, but I have changed. You can ask Connie and she'll tell you."

"What?" Abel nearly grabbed the boy. "Have you seen Connie? Is she back at the manor?"

John shook his head, "Ma would whip me if she knew that I have told you this. Connie doesn't live at the manor anymore, but I know where she is."

"Would you take me there?"

"If you want but not today, because I have to go back home before Mama finds out that I've gone. I was in the attic and saw you leaving Mr. Joel's house, so I decided to follow you. Mama thinks I have gone to the outhouse. If you can meet me at the crossroads tomorrow afternoon, I'll take you to Connie."

Abel was a bit suspicious. "Why are you helping me? Or is this a trap?"

"No, Sir. Connie is sad, and I know you were her friend. She will be happy to see you."

"Thank you, John. Now run back home before your mother gets upset with you for being away from the house. And I hope you get better."

"Yes," he rolled his sleeves back and Abel saw the fading marks. "In a few days these should have faded."

∼

The moment Captain Trent's cousin arrived later that evening Abel knew that he was looking at trouble. For some reason, she attached herself to him, and no matter how much he didn't want to be with her, she insisted on following him everywhere. It made him very uncomfortable because he didn't like her and had to pretend to be cordial to her for Mrs. Lamb's sake. And even when Captain Trent told her to give them some time so they could get some correspondence done, she insisted on standing outside the door waiting until they were finished and then she once again grabbed Abel and asked him to take a walk with her in the garden.

"I can't keep leaving Captain Trent to do the work alone when I'm his valet," he told her the next morning when he was tired of trying to hide from her. "I'm here to work and not for leisure."

"But my cousin understands that I need you."

"No, you don't," he pulled his hand away and looked at her without smiling. "Miss Landon, respect yourself. I have a lot of work to do and I can't spend time entertaining you. Please find someone else to humour you."

"But Abel..." she pouted, but he turned and walked away, leaving her with a calculating look in her eyes. He was sure that he had dealt with the whole issue once and for all.

~

Connie was dusting the furniture in the living room while Miss Tabitha and Miss Mercy were out of the house. They had gone for mid-morning high tea at a neighbour's house and she was relieved that the house was quiet. She had checked on Mr. Pitcher, and he was sleeping soundly after the doctor had administered a heavy dose of pain medication.

She heard a horse ride up to the house and knew that it couldn't be the two sisters. And she doubted that it was any of the Pitchers' visitors. Ever since they had come to live in the house after their brother got injured and was now paralyzed, they didn't get any visitors.

Connie was very careful about who she let into the house because she didn't trust anyone. Twice, adults had tried to hurt her and twice they had ended up badly hurt. And also, Miss Tabitha had warned her to never open the door for anyone unless any of them were at home.

She'd overheard Miss Tabitha and Miss Mercy talking about her stepfather. When he'd fallen down the steps of the loft, he broke his back and was now paralyzed from the waist down. Not believing them, she had asked John when he'd come to see her, visits they still kept secret and he had confirmed the fact. She felt guilty of the relief in her heart when she'd found out that her stepfather wasn't dead. The man would never hurt any other woman again. But it was still sad just thinking about him unable to walk on his own.

And as for Mr. Pitcher, he was paralyzed from the neck down, but his mouth was as cruel as ever. He never ceased to abuse her whenever she was feeding him because his sisters wouldn't feed him.

Miss Tabitha and Miss Mercy were also wont to strike her, but their words were worse. She never forgot what Abel had told her. *"Keep your head down and don't talk back."*

Sometimes the advice worked, and she evaded the two sisters, but sometimes their brother urged them on. Still, this was better than being in her parents' home. At least here no one stopped her from eating whatever food was in the house. And since the two women liked visiting their friends, they were rarely at home and the only person she had to deal with much of the time was Mr. Pitcher. And being in this house meant that her mother couldn't come visiting. For some reason, her mother avoided this house, which was just fine with Connie.

The urgent knock roused her from her reverie, and she walked to the door, heart pounding. "Who is it?"

"Connie, is that you?"

"Abel?" She couldn't believe it and quickly opened the door. She wanted to rush into his arms because he was so handsome. She hadn't seen him for nearly two years and couldn't believe how different he looked.

"What are you doing here?" She asked him, remembering that he was now engaged. Miss Tabitha had been very happy to show her the notice in the newspaper just days before.

Abel looked at the girl, no, now a young woman, that he hadn't seen for nearly two years. She had grown so much and was even more beautiful than he remembered. "Your mother said you had run away but I knew she was lying. What are you doing in this house? Are you the maid?" He looked at the rug in her hands and the broom on the floor.

"Something like that," she didn't want to tell him anything. It wasn't his business since he'd left her behind and had now moved on with his life. What had happened to him protecting her and looking out for her? Well, he was clearly looking out for and protecting the beautiful Miss Catherine Landon. Her lips tightened. "Why did you come and how did you even know that I was here?"

"It doesn't matter how I found out where you were, the thing is that I've really missed you," he approached her with outstretched arms but she sidestepped, shaking her head. "What's wrong, Connie? Aren't you happy to see me?"

"You shouldn't be here," her voice was tight.

Abel nodded, "You're angry with me because I went away and left you behind. Connie, I had no choice."

"I understand."

"No, you don't. Your mother wanted me to be thrown into prison where she could bribe someone to hurt or possibly kill me. Justice Lamb knew this and that's why he sent me to Europe with his son. But now I'm back."

"You shouldn't be here," she repeated. "Please leave me alone."

"Connie, you know I can't do that. I promised that I would always be there to protect and take care of you. Now I'm back and I have some money I've been saving for the past two years. We can go to London and live together," but she was shaking her head. "Why are you saying no?" He saw her turning pale. "What's going on, Connie?"

"You've got to leave now," Connie said when she heard voices outside signalling that Mr. Pitcher's sisters were back.

They entered the house and when they saw Abel, their eyes narrowed.

"Who is this man?" Miss Tabitha asked. "And what is he doing in our house?"

"My name is Abel Pierson, Ma'am." Abel had learned how to read people's faces and these women weren't happy. He shouldn't have come here because who knew what they would do to Connie once he left.

"You're a thief," Miss Mercy raised her voice and Abel saw trouble brewing. He rushed to the door and was out before they could call out for help.

∼

"The best way to get rid of all this nonsense that Cousin Kate is spouting is for you to return to Europe," Captain Trent told Abel a few days later. "If you stay here, she will only cause you a lot of trouble."

"Connie will never forgive me for leaving again."

"Connie is the least of your worries right now, Abel. Besides, she is a married woman living in her husband's house. You have no business interfering in her life."

"I asked her to run away with me, but she refused."

"That's because she is an honourable woman. If she ran away with you, you'd eventually lose respect for her and that is something she couldn't bear."

"But she is so unhappy in that house. Her husband and his sisters are really cruel to her. I have asked around and everyone says that she was sent to that house by her mother. Can't your father do something to help?"

Captain Trent shook his head, "My father keeps out of people's domestic issues unless someone specifically reports to him. Besides, your young woman hasn't ever come forward to place a complaint, so no one can really do anything to help her. But don't look so crestfallen. Like I told you before, if you can't do something about a matter, pray about it and seek peace in your heart."

"I still don't feel good leaving Connie behind."

"You have to leave before Cousin Kate drags you kicking and screaming down the aisle. She's told my folks that you have ruined her."

"You know that's not true."

"I know that, but if she tells her folks, they will come here, and her father is one man you don't want to deal with. The last thing I want is for anyone to make your life miserable and you've already had a lot to deal with. It has to be Europe, or you'll be in trouble. Besides that, you saw how quickly my cousin put a premature notice in the newspaper about your impending wedding. That girl is trying to trap you, and the longer you stay here the deeper in trouble you'll get."

11
A LONG WAY FROM HOME

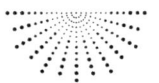

He couldn't be dead, for if he was, he wouldn't be in so much pain. Opening his eyes slowly, Abel immediately noted two things. First, it was dark, and the only light came from a small smoky lantern; and secondly, someone was chanting unintelligible things somewhere in the room where he was.

Turning his head slowly, he noticed the dark-skinned man wearing only a loin cloth walking around a small fire into which he dropped incense from time to time as he chanted.

"You are awake," the man's accent was thick. Indian! Abel noted. He stopped chanting and came and squatted beside Abel. He looked thin but surprisingly strong when he raised Abel's head and pressed a coconut shard to his mouth. "Drink," he ordered in a firm voice.

Abel opened his lips and took a sip of the foul-tasting liquid and nearly spit it out, but small hands blocked his nose, so he was forced to swallow. This treatment went on for a few more times, and his eyes smarted. Abel realised that the small hands belonged to a boy who was about four or five years old.

"Sleep," the thin man gently placed his head back on the rough pillow. He struggled to keep his eyes open but gave in to sleep with a soft sigh.

When he next woke up, it was early in the morning, and the small shack was empty. He could hear people talking outside and furtively sat up, He couldn't believe that all pain was gone, and he flexed his muscles, smiling when he realized that his whole body was still intact, and he was still in one piece with all his limbs. That had been a close call and he wondered how the rest of his unit members had fared.

That took him back to a few months before when the Crimean War had ended and he'd been at a loss of what to do. Connie was always on his mind, and he didn't want to go back to her emptyhanded. As he was still considering what to do with his life now that the war was over, one of the sergeants who had been Captain Trent's friends and who had looked out for him when he returned had called him over.

"I know you want to go back home but I have a proposition for you," Sergeant Wycliffe Burns had pulled him aside. "I'd like you to listen to me without saying anything and then have a day or two to think about it. Your unit will soon be shipping back out of this place and I'd like an answer before that happens."

And Abel had listened as the man extolled the merits of joining the British East India Trading Company as one of its soldiers. "But I'm not all that qualified to be a soldier," Abel had protested.

"Consider this more training for you, Son," the forty-something-year-old man told him. "Going to India to look after the interests of the Queen over there is an honour.

What's more, the pay is really good, much better than what you would get as a regular soldier. So, what do you say?"

It hadn't taken Abel long to decide. He'd seen what poverty could do and never wanted to be helpless again. If going to India would enable him to make something of himself then he was ready to do so. What's more, Sergeant Burns told him he could sign on for only one year and then decide whether to continue being a soldier or take up his discharge papers.

His unit had been on the way from Calcutta to Delhi when a section of the Indian soldiers led an armed revolt against their British counterparts and tried to make it into a war for India's independence. Abel's unit was ambushed, and the last thing he remembered was running into the thick forest; then he lost his memory. He had no idea if his colleagues were all right, but he highly doubted it. They'd clearly been led into an ambush by one of the Indian officers, and then they were outnumbered.

A sound alerted him to the fact that he was no longer alone. When he looked toward the door, he noticed two small boys who seemed to be twins and aged about five years. Their faces were so identical, and the dark eyes were full of curiosity and he smiled at them. He remembered that one of them was the one who had held his nose as his father forced him to drink the herbs, but he couldn't immediately tell which one it was.

It was clear that these folks didn't intend him any harm, for if they had, they wouldn't have treated him so he could get better.

"Hello," he said and realized that his voice was hoarse.

One of the boys grinned at him, then dashed back out while the other remained at the doorway staring at him.

"Papa," the running boy was shouting and then speaking rapidly in Hindi.

A few minutes later, the man he'd kept seeing when he woke up in brief interludes walked in. His hands were clasped in front of him and he bowed.

"Good morning,"

Abel smiled, "You speak English?"

"Little, little," the man was shaking his head and nodding at the same time, a motion Abel had noticed most Indians did. It wasn't clear whether they were saying yes or no, and it always amused him when they did that. Of course, it had confused him and his fellow British officers because they had no idea if the Indians were agreeing to or rejecting whatever they were telling them.

He got to his feet and tried to take a step forward, but his legs nearly gave in.

"Sorry, sorry," his host was immediately at his side.

"I need to go outside," Abel whispered as the man supported him and took him to an outhouse where he completed his business. It was a shaky shack, and Abel feared that he might fall inside, and it was a relief to step out without any mishaps. He didn't like the smell that his body was emitting and more than anything he wished he could take a bath. As if his host had read his mind, the man took his hand.

"You come," his host led him down a path and they soon came to a stream that was bubbling merrily.

"Mama Ganga," the man pointed at the water.

"Huh?" Abel looked at him in confusion.

"Ganges River, Mama Ganga," the man bowed his head.

"Ah," Abel nodded, the River Ganges.

"You wash."

Abel needed no second bidding. Sitting on a partly immersed rock, he washed himself with hard soap, but it didn't smell too terrible. His host, who told him his name was Thomas Prakash, gave him a change of clothing and took his own tattered ones away. Abel doubted that he would ever see his uniform again, but for now he was just happy to be clean and alive.

Once cleaned and fed on rice and lentils, Abel once more stretched himself out on the mat and slept.

∽

"What are we searching for?" Abel asked the two boys who were darting in and out of the caves, stones in their hands.

"Kargosh," the younger twin, Anuj said, "Kargosh."

"Whatever that is," Abel muttered. It was really hot, and he was sweating. But he was glad that Prakash, his host, had given him a loose-fitting shirt, and he also wore a loin cloth. Still the shirt was plastered on his back as he felt the sweat trickling down between his shoulders.

"Kargosh," Lucas Anuj, the oldest twin emerged from one of the caves, holding a hare by its ears, and Abel smiled. So they were hunting for wild hares now.

Since he was still too weak to till the land as his host Prakash, his wife Reena and three daughters did, Abel accompanied the twins into the caves to hunt for rats and hares. The family was so poor, but Abel was touched that they were willing to share their food with him. From his conversations with Prakash he had found out the name of this village.

Ramantra Village, which was comprised of three families; Prakash and his two cousins Samjibhai and Laljibhai. Among the three families, his hosts was the smallest because he only had five children. His cousins had more than ten living children each, and they had even buried some in infancy.

The small boys amazed him with their fearlessness and soon he too was darting in and out of the caves with them. Abel had lost count of how long he'd been with this generous family as the days just rolled into each other. His body was healing well, and he was feeling stronger, yet he was somehow reluctant to return to active duty. According to his heart, he was done with war and being a soldier, and all he wanted was to go back to England and start his life all over again. And he would win Connie away from that old man she was married to; it didn't matter what he had to do to get her back.

So he was happy to hunt for kargosh, hares, with the young boys, and they would then spend the rest of the day swimming in the river. It was during one such excursion that Anuj emerged with his pouch full of pebbles. When they got home and were seated outside the house waiting for dinner to be served, the boys started playing with the stones.

At first Abel took no notice of their game, but something about those small pink pebbles pulled at him. He noticed them sparkling in the light of the fire that Reena had lit, and he blinked rapidly.

"Anuj, let me see," he held out his hand and the boy dropped a few of the small stones into his hand. Abel stared disbelievingly at the stones and then the boys, "Do you know what these are?" He asked them. They didn't understand him very well, but Prakash chose to join them then, "Mr. Prakash, do you know what these are?"

The man's head shook and nodded at the same time, "Playing stones."

"No these are semi-precious stones."

"Huh, stones the boys play with. Many stones, many children find and play with."

"No," Abel didn't know how to explain his findings, "This stone is the rose quartz. It's a semi- precious stone that is said to make very beautiful jewellery."

"Gold?"

"No, it's a precious stone that isn't gold. The rose quartz," Abel was really excited. He'd seen plenty of these stones in some stores in Delhi and also back at a jewellery store in London.

"Where did they find these stones?" He asked Prakash, who turned to his sons and spoke to them in Hindi. They responded excitedly and he looked at Abel.

"They say the stones were in one of the caves where they caught hares."

"Can they take me there tomorrow?"

"Of course, any time you want."

When Abel saw the pile of pink crystal stones, he thought he was dreaming. They were spread all over the floor of the inner cave in small piles. Anuj had brought a small tin lantern with which they were able to see their way. Abel gasped as he knelt down before the small stones and started gathering as many of them as he could. This was immense wealth, and he wondered that no one had discovered it. But then this was a remote village, and he even wondered how Prakash and his family had found him so far off the path. Folding the front of his loin cloth, he gathered as many as he could carry. Once back at home, he sat down to assess them.

His host family stared at him as if he were insane, the three daughters and their mother giggling from time to time as they pointed at him. It was clear to him that these people had no idea of the immense wealth that was on their land.

For the next few weeks, Abel and the boys gathered the precious stones. He had asked for Prakash's permission to dig a hole in the room where he slept in. He spread his sleeping mat over it just in case any curious strangers passed by. Each passing day he added to the pile and he longed for the Rebellion to end so he could return. The war didn't touch on this small village, something for which Abel was glad. He was tired of seeing needless deaths. But Prakash had told him to be very careful because once in a while rebels passed through the village. As an Englishman his life was in danger because they wouldn't hesitate to capture him for ransom.

Finally, Prakash brought him the news he'd been hoping for.

"The British were in the town square," he said.

"What were they doing?"

"The war is over," his host looked at him with sad eyes, "You go home?"

"Yes, I'll go home but I will be back. You were so kind to me and I will return to build you a nice house."

Prakash merely smiled, looking at the sad shack that was his family home. Abel could see that he didn't believe him.

"Where did you learn to speak such good English?"

"The priest, Father Piers, he teach me English. I teach him Hindi, and he teach me English. Then he baptized me, and I am now called Thomas. My wife is Joanne."

"You have Christians here?" Abel asked in surprise. He hadn't once been taken to or asked to accompany the family to any church.

"Huh! My father, Christian and grandfather Christian."

"I didn't think there would be any Christians this far in the villages of India."

"Christianity came to India in the first century. The Apostle Thomas left Jerusalem after the Dispersion and travelled for many miles to India."

"I never knew that at all." He observed Prakash's three daughters who were old enough for marriage.

Prakash noticed his gaze, "My daughters cannot get married."

"Why not? I have noticed that there are many young men in this area. Marriage should be fairly easy for them because they are pretty girls. Why not just ask some good boys to offer for your daughters?"

"No dowry," Prakash shook his head, "I am too poor. If my sons were older, they would find girls with good dowry. Then my daughters would be married."

Abel had been thinking of another way of expressing his gratitude to his hosts. This family had taken him in when he was badly wounded and nursed him back to health. Though they were very poor, they shared everything they had and what's more, together with his close neighbours, had kept him hidden from the rebels.

"I will be back," Abel said, "And when I return, your daughters will be married."

"They will be married when the Lord wills it," Prakash said.

∼

It took Abel nearly three months to settle down in Bombay. He had thought of going to Delhi but decided on Bombay because it was the largest city and that was where the headquarters of the British East India Company and his employer, were. The first thing he did was to resign his commission from the British Army and cited poor health as his reason for quitting the army. Because he'd been missing in action and presumed dead for nearly three months, it wasn't too difficult for him to get his discharge papers, and Captain Trent, whom he communicated with as soon as he left Ramastra, also put in a good word for him.

His friends back in the village had sewed the precious stones into his clothes, laughing all the while as they thought he was demented for placing high value on children's playing stones. He'd simply smiled, and when he got to Bombay, he was very careful about finding buyers for his precious cargo. Bombay was a very busy city and even though there were many businessmen who were English like himself, he was still very cautious about his safety. Though the Indian War of Rebellion was over, tensions were still high, and both sides still looked at each other suspiciously. But that didn't stop him from also finding some good friends who helped him sell his stones, though he was very careful, having been taught all caution by Captain Trent Lamb.

But finally, the day came when he could return to Ramastra village to see his friends. This time he returned as a victor and when his hosts saw him, they were overcome with emotions.

"You came back," Prakash said, bowing himself low as did his wife and children.

"And we are going to find good husbands for your three girls," he said. "But first, I promised to build you a nice house, your neighbours too. Your three families were good to me and I want to repay you."

"It is enough that you came back and brought us all these gifts."

Abel smiled. While in Bombay he'd become friends with the jeweller who bought his rose quartz stones. Abel had asked him all about the rites observed during Indian wedding ceremonies and what was required. So he'd bought many saris and gold for the girls and their mother, as well as for Prakash's other relatives. It touched him when the small village decided to throw a large celebration in his honour, and one of Prakash's cousins even offered him his thirty-two-year-old daughter as a wife.

"I have a woman waiting for me in England," he told Samjibhai, who shook his head with much regret. But the man was soon appeased when Abel said he was willing to settle dowry on Seeta so she could also find a husband.

Once families from neighbouring villages heard that Prakash's daughters and cousins now had attractive dowries, it didn't take long for the nearly ten girls, including Seeta, to find good husbands. There was much rejoicing in the once poverty-stricken village as Abel not only built good houses for the three families, he also purchased cows, goats and sheep for the families so they could have a means of livelihood.

"You have made me a very happy man," Prakash said with tears in his eyes as they watched his three daughters and seven nieces performing the required marriage rites with their suitors. "My sons-in-law are good, hard-working men, and my daughters and nieces will prosper."

"May they prosper and live long lives," Abel agreed.

"But you don't have a wife?"

Abel smiled sadly, "There is a girl back in England, as I told your brother," he said. "When I return, I will ask her to be my wife."

"Is she waiting for you after all these years? You told me you were in the war in Europe before coming to India. What if you find that someone else has married her already?"

Abel thought about Connie and the fact that she was married to Henry Pitcher. He nodded, "Yes, she is waiting for me," he said with a bright smile even as his heart hoped that this time Connie would truly be his.

"I wish you all good blessings and many children," Prakash said.

"May your words be prophecy indeed," he said.

12

WORLDS APART

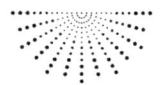

Connie noticed that Henry's health was failing, but he was just as snappish as usual. Four years of being his 'wife' in name only meant that she was now well acquainted with his moods and various mood swings.

"Are you really all right?" She asked him one morning when she noticed that he was swallowing with much difficulty. She'd made him a breakfast of soft oatmeal porridge and put a lot of milk in the mixture, but he was struggling to swallow it. "Is it too hot for you," and she blew over the spoon before moving it to his lips. He turned his head away and she sighed, looking at him with much compassion in her eyes.

Over the years as she'd lived in this house and withstood abuse from him and his sisters something had broken within her. Instead of seeing him as someone who threatened her, she saw him as a broken vessel that was to be pitied. The only thing that worried her was that he had started moving his left hand, and often he used it to strike out at her. She was always careful to sit on his right side because he couldn't turn himself, and she watched out for the mobile hand.

"What are you staring at me for, woman?" He growled at her, raising his left hand like he wanted to strike her, but she was out of reach.

She wanted to feel angry at him for the way he and his sisters had treated her for the past four years but found only pity in her heart. Bitterness of spirit was a terrible thing, she thought. The man was wealthy, not as much as her own parents, but he wanted for nothing. Yet he was one of the most miserable men she'd ever had the misfortune to meet. And it wasn't just because of his accident, but she had once eavesdropped on his own sisters when they were talking about how mean and miserly he was. All his property was controlled by his solicitor, a man Connie didn't trust for one moment. Mr. Barnes had shifty eyes and he always treated her like she was an fool whenever he came to the house. And he was the only one who called her 'Mrs. Pitcher' though she always felt like he was mocking her.

He held tight onto Mr. Pitcher's purse strings and insisted on every penny he disbursed being accounted for, which didn't sit very well with Miss Tabitha and Miss Mercy. Connie really didn't care about Mr. Pitcher's money because she didn't feel like she deserved it. But it surprised her when once in a while, Mr. Barnes would bring her a dress or two, not brand new, of course, but it was the thought that counted.

"Open the curtains and then fetch me some chicken broth," he barked at her and as she walked to the window, forgetting about his left hand. "Go and prepare me chicken broth and bring it quickly. And make sure you don't burn it. You're just a worthless woman and I don't even know what you're still doing in this house."

Lips tightened, Connie picked up the tray with the half-eaten oatmeal and hobbled out of the room. She stood outside his bedroom and forced the tears to recede, even though her heart hurt terribly. *How could a man be so wicked even when he was an invalid?* she wondered. *Were some people just born with blackened hearts and seared consciences or did they grow into them?*

While she prepared the broth from the half chicken left over from the previous day's dinner, she ignored Henry's sisters, who were watching her with snickers on their faces. But at least they didn't say anything as she carried broth to Mr. Pitcher.

The moment he tasted a spoonful, he swiped at the bowl and the hot broth flooded her skirt. Mercifully it was made of thick wool and absorbed the hot liquid else she would have been badly scalded. Some of the broth spilled on his pillow forming a large patch and the rest on the floor.

"No matter how dark it is, morning shall come," she murmured as she wiped the tears away. "Keep my head down and don't answer back."

"Change my pillow because I want to sleep right now and then get out of my presence."

But Connie said nothing. She would never give him the satisfaction of knowing how much his words hurt her. Because she never left the house or compound, she had no idea where Abel was, but she often thought of him. For some reason for the past two months or so, her brother had stopped coming to visit her. She missed him because they had grown close and she thought that maybe her mother had found out about his visits and forbidden him from coming to see her.

∽

Something woke Connie up two nights later and she sat up quickly, listening with a pounding heart. She could hear footsteps, hurrying past her door and she wondered what was going on.

"Hurry, Tabitha," Mercy sounded like she was in a panic and Connie frowned.

"Should I wake Constance up?" Tabitha asked.

"No, just bring me the water first. We'll get to her later."

Connie got out of bed and pulled on her frock then walked to the door and drew the bolt back. She could hear the cocks crowing in the distance and knew that morning would soon be here. What was going on? When she opened the door, she saw people standing outside Mr. Pitcher's bedchamber. It was Troy the stableman and Mr. Barnes, and she wondered that the latter was here in the house this early. But she shrugged, putting those questions aside and moving toward them.

"What is going on?" she asked no one in particular as she drew closer and peeped into Henry's bedchamber. Someone had lit many candles bathing the room in great light. Mr. Pitcher wouldn't like that at all, and she was the one who would bear the brunt of his insults. He insisted on every room only having one candle, yet his bedchamber now looked like the altar at a church during Christmas time.

"Don't just stand there gaping at me like a fish out of water," Tabitha caught sight of her, "Do something." The older woman had a small dish in her hands and was wiping Mr. Pitcher's brow with a piece of cloth. "You should be helping and not just looking at me."

Connie had no idea what she was supposed to do but before she could take a step into Mr. Pitcher's bedchamber Miss Mercy stopped her.

"Don't bother," she sneered at Connie, "You should be happy now."

"Why should I be happy?"

"Don't pretend to be concerned now and stop being a hypocrite. You wanted my brother dead and gone. Well, you can put on your hat and dance, for Henry is no more."

Connie felt weakness invade her whole body and she sagged against the wall. Henry was dead. The nightmare of being his mistreated wife was over. She didn't know whether to laugh or cry.

Being a kind-hearted person, she felt compassion but also pity. The man had been mean and almost sadistic while he lived, and she wondered why he had chosen to live a bitter life when he could have been so happy. He'd seemed to thrive on being cruel and she forced herself to step into his bedchamber and see for herself. It was like she was dreaming and would wake up to find that he was still alive, and his mouth spewing insults at her as usual.

Ignoring the hisses from his sisters, she approached the bed and looked down at the grey face. Even in death his thin lips were twisted as if he was in pain.

"Go in peace," she murmured, turning away.

But Miss Tabitha walked to the bedroom door and slammed it shut so it was just the three of them and Mr. Pitcher's body. The solicitor protested but was ignored as the door was shut in his face.

Connie looked longingly at the closed door, but Miss Tabitha shook her head.

"You will stand here and listen to what I have to say," she said slowly. "My brother is dead, and I want you to get it out of your head that you are his widow. We happen to know that your marriage was never consummated so you can't claim to have been his wife in the true sense of the word."

Connie felt very tired. It had been a long four years, and she felt completely drained.

"What do you want, Miss Tabitha?" she asked wearily, "I'm very tired…"

Tabitha's face was contorted, "How dare you stand there telling me that you're tired when my beloved brother has just died? I could smite you so hard that you won't be able to walk for weeks. But that would only make you a burden to us and we want you gone from this house."

"Where will I go?" Connie asked fearfully. Many times, she had prayed for a way out of this house, but now that the chance had come, she found that she was terrified of leaving. This prison had also been her sanctuary in some way, and now she would once again be homeless.

"I don't care where you end up because you are not needed here anymore."

Connie had heard enough. She walked to the door, "Please open the door and let me leave."

"Not before I have finished with you."

Connie raised her eyes to Miss Tabitha, but she refused to break down before the cold, unfeeling selfish woman.

"You will receive nothing from my brother's estate," Miss Tabitha hissed. "And you know what the justice in all this is, that you will forever have nothing."

Connie clenched her fists, "I have no desire to claim anything from your brother," she said with false bravado. "After all, when he was alive, I claimed nothing. I don't need anything upon his death except my freedom."

"Your mother thought you would be a rich woman by bringing you here to marry my brother but all you brought him was back luck," the scorn was dripping from Miss Mercy's lips. "You're nothing but an opportunist and a gold digger, and the sooner you leave the better for all of us before you bring us more tragedy. Your wickedness has brought punishment to you because even if you leave this house, you'll never find a man to marry you," she laughed, a cruel sound. "I know you've always had this secret desire to be married to that worthless man who married the society belle and then disappeared to war. Just so you know, I was at the grocery store the other day and overheard Mrs. Lamb telling Mr. Shepherd that Abel Pierson was killed in some war in India. His unit was attacked by rebel Indians and they were all killed, and their bodies burnt."

"What?" Connie thought she would swoon. Abel was dead.

The two women jeered at her, but it was Miss Tabitha who spoke. "Yes, the man you thought you would leave our brother for is dead, so you have nothing now. This is just reward for your selfishness when my brother did so much and saved you from a fate worse than death."

Connie stiffened. She had been abused, beaten and humiliated in this household for four long years. And she had never once fought back. She had no desire to exchange bitter words with these women because she knew that they were looking for an excuse to strike her. But she wouldn't give them the chance to do so.

She was free! Henry's death had freed her from this prison, and she would not spend a day longer in this horrible house.

She shook her head and brushed past Miss Tabitha, threw the door open and hastened to her bedchamber. She ignored the people in the corridor and bolted the door from the inside.

It was getting lighter outside, and she wanted to be gone before more neighbours came, possibly her mother, too. She was eighteen years old now and would never allow anyone to enslave her again, so she needed to leave before her mother decided to come and force her back to Malone Manor. Looking around at the sparsely furnished bedroom that had been her domain for four years, she finally allowed a smile to break on her face.

Connie then sobered up as she thought about the future. Though she had nowhere to go, returning to her mother was out of the question. In the four years since she had come to Mr. Pitcher's house, her mother had never once set foot here to see her. Not that she had any desire to see the woman who had sold her to a man three times her age.

No, she shook her head, chewing desperately on her lower lip. But how was she supposed to leave this house without knowing where to go? And she had no money because not once had she been paid for her labours.

Then she remembered something. The first day when she had woken up in this room and Mr. Pitcher had tried to attack her, he had stumbled and fallen. As he was being carried out of her bedchamber after his injury, he'd dropped some coins which her brother had found and handed over to her. Even though it was just three or four farthings the coins were precious to her and she had sewn them into the lining of her mattress. The coins were still there, and she quickly tore the old mattress, uncaring that down was flying all over the place.

Three farthings! She looked around, and since she had nothing of value she wished to carry with her, she unbolted the door and walked down the stairs and out of the imposing prison.

This is how prisoners who have been released must feel, she thought, as she hobbled down the short driveway, never once turning around to look at the house she had left.

∼

Abel looked at the two women who were observing him with interest and he nearly laughed out loud. The last time he'd been here they had called him a thief, and he'd escaped before they could shout out. Had he been caught, he was sure they would have demanded that he be lynched. Yet now their stations in life had changed, and he was looking down on them with pity in his eyes.

He'd arrived from India a month ago and because of setting up his business in London hadn't been able to travel to Ritter's Village sooner. Yet as soon as he'd set foot in this village, the first person he wanted to see was Connie, though it took him a further two days to visit her.

As a soldier, Captain Trent had taught him how to scout the land before approaching enemy territory and he'd decided to find out all he could about Mr. Henry Pitcher. The story he was told was more amusing than sad and he'd come away shaking his head.

After Henry Pitcher's death about a month ago, his solicitor, a certain Mr. Barnes, had seduced the two sisters and deceived them into signing over whatever inheritance their brother had left them. According to Henry Pitcher's will, so Abel was informed, his two sisters got an equal share. The crafty Mr. Barnes had played the sisters against each other and even supposedly married the older one. Once he had Mr. Pitcher's wealth in his hands, he'd disappeared, and no one had seen or heard from him since. The worst of it was that he'd sold the house as well as the land on which it stood, thus rendering the two sisters homeless. They were forced to seek a cottage on someone's estate to rent.

Abel had come prepared to negotiate with Henry Pitcher for Connie's freedom. Four years was a long time, and he was sure she would probably have two or three children by now. But it didn't matter because Connie was his woman, the love of his life. He had purposed that he would take her away from the man who didn't deserve her. Only he had found out that Mr. Pitcher had been crippled four years ago, on the very day that Connie had come into this household. And the man was now dead and there were no issues in the marriage.

Then he thought about the time when he had come to see Connie and she'd asked him to leave. She hadn't looked like someone who was happily married and yet she wouldn't run away with him. But Captain Trent's words came back to mind; Connie was an honourable woman and had stayed with her husband until his death. But where had she disappeared to? He couldn't believe that he'd missed her by a month.

"Well?" he asked, gritting his teeth and barely holding onto his temper, "Where is Miss Constance?"

"That woman is full of evil," Miss Tabitha dubbed delicately at her eyes. "My brother's body was barely cold before some fancy carriage pulled up at the front door, and off she went."

"Fancy carriage? Whose?" While the story didn't sound at all true, Abel was still concerned, "Whose carriage did she leave in?"

The woman shrugged, "My brother was an invalid from the day that woman stepped into this house, and we don't know what she did to him. As if that wasn't enough, she took many lovers and some she even brought to this house. That is the reason we came to live here so we could curtail her dishonourable ways. But she is clever, is Miss Constance Baker. Now I believe she is fleecing some poor old man for his wealth like she did to our brother."

"Is that right?" Abel looked around the small dilapidated cottage. He shook his head as his gaze once again fixed on the two women. "I have never seen more wicked people than the two of you. The news of your cruelty has spread far and wide. Everyone knows that you chased Connie out of here so you could inherit your brother's wealth, for some conniving man to fleece you of your ill-gotten gains," he shook his head. "This is your destiny and just reward," he walked to the door, "And just so you know, my good friend owns the land on which this cottage stands."

Their faces paled at the implication of his words.

"Mercy please," Miss Tabitha begged. "See I'm with child and have nowhere else to go. That man deceived me and then he ran away with all my money," she said bitterly.

"You should have at least showed mercy to that poor young woman when she lived in your home. And even now you still lie about her. What kind of women are you?"

"We are very sorry and just ask for your mercy. We have been punished enough," Miss Mercy was weeping.

"Blessed are the merciful, said our Lord, for they will receive mercy, and, dear ladies, cursed are the wicked for they will reap the fruits of their wickedness."

He slammed the door which shook the cottage. But once he sat in his carriage and told the driver to leave, he was a worried man. The one thing he knew, Connie would never have gone back to her mother's house or his parents would have mentioned it when he'd visited them the previous day. So where was she, and if she had boarded some fancy carriage as the two women alleged, where had the person taken her and who was it?

13
THE TIDE WILL TURN

London was so different from Cambridge, and Connie was amazed at the fast-paced life of the large city. Having alighted at Euston, she slowly walked out of the station, wondering where she would go. It was early afternoon and the train journey had taken four hours from Ritter's Village to London.

As soon as she stepped out of the station, she noticed an elderly couple standing on the pavement on her side. Their clothes, though tattered, seemed clean and they were holding hands, clearly unable to cross because of the carts, buggies and carriages that rushed past them in both directions. People jostled them, uncaring that they were elderly, and she felt compassion well up within her heart.

"Do you need help crossing the street?" she approached them and made sure to stand at a respectful distance so as not to intimidate them.

"Would you be so kind as to help us get across?" the man asked. They looked to be in their seventies.

"Yes, I will help you, but I can only take one of you at a time. Will that be all right?"

"Thank you, child," the woman's voice trembled, "We were afraid that we might have to stand here until late in the evening.

It took about half an hour to get them both safely across the street.

"You seem to have just arrived on the train," the woman said, "Do you have a place to go? We are sorry that we took up your time and delayed you from reaching your destination." She held out a penny. "Please accept this for your troubles."

Connie shook her head, "Thank you but I can't accept payment for doing a good deed. I am happy to help you. And yes, it's true that I have just arrived from Cambridge and I was wondering if I could find some cheap but good lodgings somewhere around here. Then tomorrow I can begin searching for work to do."

"No, child," the woman placed a gentle hand on her arm, "You have been very kind to us, and we wouldn't want you to get into trouble. London is a frightening place and not safe for a little one like you alone. Why don't you come home with us?"

"I wouldn't want to impose on you, "Connie imagined that the poor couple probably lived in a shack in one of the slums of the city. They looked poor and yet the woman had been willing to give her a penny.

'You wouldn't be imposing on us. We want you to be safe," and thus persuaded, Connie held both their hands, gently leading them home.

She was surprised when their home turned out to be a two-storied town house in the poorer part of Euston just down the road from the station.

"You have a nice house," she told them as she waited for the old man to open the door and then he ushered his wife and Connie inside. "I must confess that I was worried you would be living in a one-roomed shack or something like that. Please forgive me for my wrong deductions."

"This house has been in my family for decades," the man said, pride in his voice, "But as you can see, the windows were broken by vandals and we had to board them up to keep unwanted pests and squatters out. There's a good man who watches the house for us when we are out." He looked at Connie. "My good name is Robert Mather, and this here is my lovely wife of fifty years, Claudia Mather."

∽

They shared a simple supper of fresh bread, cheese and hot broth which Connie helped Mrs. Mather to prepare. After Connie had washed the dishes and tidied the kitchen, Mrs. Mather showed her to a back room in which was a narrow cot. What made Connie smile was the thick quilt on the bed.

"You can live here with us for as long as you want," Mrs. Mather said, "This used to be our granddaughter's bedroom but she got married and moved to Scotland," the woman looked sad, "She never writes nor has she visited us for the past ten years. We worry that she might be dead or worse, being mistreated, and has no way of letting us know. I just wish Juliana would come back home to us," she wiped a tear away.

"I'm so sorry."

"We are decent folk, not thieves or bad people, just old. We both worked and took care of Juliana from when she was little. It was our dream and hope that she would take care of us in our old age. But then she met a smooth-talking man who married her and took her to Scotland," she sniffed softly. "I just pray that she is happy and well.

Connie didn't know what to say, "Do you rent out the rooms upstairs to tenants?"

"No, they are in a deplorable state and besides, no one wants to live in a windowless house. My Robert and I go to Euston Station every day to beg. We get a little that enables us to live."

An idea came to Connie's mind, "Can I work for you? I can clean and cook and then walk you to and from the station," she looked around the room, "This is a nice house to live in."

Mrs. Mather laughed softly, "You must be really desperate to think that this is a nice house. Why would a sweet and beautiful girl like you want to spend your life taking care of two old doddering folks? You could find a good man to marry you."

Connie felt sadness come over her. "I can never marry," she said, shaking her head. "The man I loved left me and the last I heard about him, he'd married someone else and then he went abroad and died out there."

"You poor child," Mrs. Mather shook her head sadly, "My Robert fought in the Napoleonic war decades ago. He went to war as a young man of twenty and left me with two children," she wiped her eyes. "He was in Paris and I got news that he was dead. It nearly killed me, and I suffered a miscarriage. But he came back and we have had fifty-five years of a happy life together. You will find someone who will wipe away your tears."

"I doubt it, but you are kind for saying that. So, can I stay? I promise that I won't be a bother to you."

"You can live with us," then Mrs. Mather frowned. "I noticed that you are wincing as you walk and then you limp also. What happened to your leg? Were you in some accident or were you born with a problem?"

Connie looked down and shuddered. "Mrs. Mather, it's a very long story and I promise that I will tell it to you one day. But like you, I'm not a thief or a wicked person. When I left Cambridge, my desire was to come to London and find some work to do so that I can earn my living. I promise that I won't give you any trouble."

"Don't fret, dear child. This world is full of a lot of troubles as our dear Lord Jesus said, but you shall overcome them at the last. Nothing lasts forever and especially not the bad things, so continue to hold on to hope and faith. Someday soon you shall have a reason to smile and be happy again. And it's alright, you can tell me your story whenever you're ready."

"Thank you."

∽

Faraway in Ritter's Village

"You look very pretty, Ladies," the two men told Mary and Anne Baker who giggled, covering their lips and fluttering their eyelashes at them.

"Do you really think so?" Seventeen-year-old Mary smiled at the taller of the two men.

"Oh yes, you really are."

The two sisters had been invited to a neighbour's house down the road. The Smiths were holding a small dinner party to meet the man their eldest daughter Amanda wanted to get married to. The two men were friends of the family, as they had introduced themselves.

"You both look so grown up," the second man said, exchanging an odd look with his friend but the two girls were too caught up in the moment to pay attention to the men's clandestine signals. "Would you like to see the garden? Mrs. Smith has planted some pretty roses and I'd like to pluck one and slip it into your beautiful, thick hair," he told sixteen-year-old Anne.

The two girls, who had been brought up believing that they were more beautiful than their peers, unwisely followed the two men into the darkness like lambs to the slaughter.

Hours later, the two girls practically crawled to one of the carriages and begged the driver to take them home. He was an elderly man and seeing their broken looks, didn't ask any questions. The girls held each other, weeping silently all the while silently praying that they wouldn't meet their mother when they got home. They had been through the worst four hours of their lives and felt deep shame at the way they had allowed themselves to be taken advantage of by two smooth-talking men. Worse was when they both realised that they didn't even know the names of their assailants.

But six weeks later when Mrs. Dinah Baker heard the two girls retching, she suspected that things weren't as they should be. And with tears pouring down their faces, the two girls recounted what had happened to them at the Smiths' tea party.

"Do you know the names of the men who did this to you?"

"No Mama," Mary whispered brokenly.

"What kind of trouble is this you've brought on this family? What shame and how will I hold up my head before my peers?" Mrs. Baker shouted at her two frightened daughters. She ignored the incessantly ringing bell and watched as Grant rushed to open the door.

"I am deeply ashamed of the two of you. We have brought you up to be morally upright and yet when some idiot smiles at you, you forget all the values that we've taught you. You're just sixteen and seventeen and are going to be unwed mothers. Well, I'm not ready to be a grandmother and you need to think about what you're going to do with those children."

She turned when she heard heavy footsteps and a smartly dressed man followed Grant into the living room. He looked familiar but her mind was too full of the shocking news that her daughters had just relayed to her.

"Good morning, Dinah," the man gave her a strange smile. "Do you remember me?" He didn't even wait for an invitation but crossed the living room and sat down, placing one leg over the knee of the other. His large arms were stretched across the couch. "It is nice to see you after all these years."

～

Abel had no idea why he dismissed his carriage and decided to walk down Euston Road. He wanted to buy a go-down close to the railway station and had just finished a promising meeting. Once the men carried out the necessary repairs on the building, he would complete the sale.

It was hard to believe that just months ago he'd been a very poor soldier. Now he was a landowner and also a landlord. He intended to go into business with Trent Lamb and they were going to be shipping commodities from India, hence the need for a warehouse. And they would then distribute their products as far as trains went in all directions of the country.

Yes, he thought, the lines are fallen to me in good places, but he was still sad, would he ever find his Connie?

"I will search the world for you, my darling," he whispered as he stopped and prepared to cross the road.

Euston Road was its usual busy self, and he noticed three beggars huddled under an old building. Before his time in India, he would have passed them without a second thought. But seeing those three reminded him of Prakash and his family. They looked like a family and he stared as the young lady hobbled around making sure her parents were all right, and the little scene touched him.

He waited for two more carriages to go by, then quickly crossed the road. Tossing a few pennies into their bowl didn't seem right so he reached for his wallet and extracted a five-pound note.

"Here you go Miss…Connie?" Abel rubbed his eyes to make sure he wasn't dreaming.

"Abel?" Connie thought she was seeing a ghost. She turned so pale that he got really worried. He rushed to her, ready to hold her in case she fell. But she reached up a trembling hand and touched his cheek. "It's really you."

"Yes, my love, it's really me." He couldn't believe it. What were the chances that his choice to walk instead of ride in his carriage would bring him to the woman he loved and had been searching for all these months? "It is a miracle because I never thought I would ever see you again."

Abel ignored the curious looks of passers-by, who were no doubt wondering how and why a finely dressed gentleman would be hugging a street beggar. But he didn't care. He had found his love and that was all that mattered.

"I was told you died in India," Connie said, recalling the malicious glee on Miss Tabitha and Miss Mercy's faces when they were conveying the news to her. "That your unit was ambushed by rebel Indians and everybody was killed, and your bodies burnt to ashes."

Abel wanted to tell her everything, but it wasn't the place to do it. He smiled at the couple who were looking at them with avid curiosity. Connie remembered her manners, "Abel, this is Mr. Robert and his wife Mrs. Claudia. I live with them now," she felt her face flaming because of shame. Then she shrugged the shame off. Begging was better than some of the other things young women like her were doing to survive on the harsh streets of London.

"Mr. Robert, Mrs. Claudia, this is Abel."

"This must be the man you thought had died," Claudia nodded slowly. She turned to Abel, "You have a fine one here, young man. She has never looked at another man and promised that she would remain a spinster for the rest of her life. She must love you very much."

Abel's look softened further when he looked at Connie's flaming face, "And I love her so much. It's a miracle I have found her after searching for her for these past few months." He rubbed her hand, "I would like the three of you to come to my house so we can talk. Out here we're drawing some unwanted attention."

∽

Connie caught her breath in a gasp when she saw Abel's house for the first time. It was a new brownstone on Sloan Road, Chelsea Street. In the nearly four months that she had lived with Mr. and Mrs. Mather in London, this was one part of the city that she'd never stepped into. First, she would have been glared at by guards and a constable or two might have arrested her for trespassing in the elite neighbourhood.

Abel's house was smaller than her parents' and even Mr. Pitcher's houses, but it was so much more splendid. She stared at the marble columns that held up the front portico. The inside was even more impressive, and Abel smiled when he saw Connie's face. "My darling, this is all for you."

"For me? I don't understand."

Abel saw Mr. and Mrs. Mather seated on one of the new couches and rang the small golden bell. After they were served with tea and dainty pastries, he sat down next to Connie and took her hands.

"When I returned from India about four months ago, the first place I went to was that awful house where you lived with those terrible people," his lips thinned, "It's a wonder you survived in that house. But I was determined that I would pay anything to get you away from that man. Believe me, even if you had ten children, I would have taken you away from Henry Pitcher. It's just a good thing he was already dead."

"He died four months ago, and his sisters chased me away. They wanted to inherit all he owned."

Abel grinned, "Well whatever they inherited, it wasn't much."

"What do you mean? He always said that he had a lot of money."

"Whatever that man left was all stolen by his lawyer. The man deceived Miss Tabitha into marrying him and then when he got hold of Mr. Pitcher's wealth, he disappeared. He even sold the house and the grounds on which it stood, and Mr. Pitcher's sisters lost their home. They are now living in an old dilapidated shack and barely have anything to eat."

"That's really sad."

"Sad," Abel's look was incredulous, "After all they did to you, you still feel sorry for them?"

"No one deserves to be in poverty."

"They do, and that's how I feel," his tone was firm, and Connie didn't want to argue with him.

14
THE DAY THE RAIN CAME DOWN

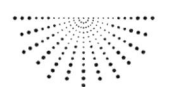

Connie slept deeply and awoke the next morning to the sweet sound of birds chirping merrily just outside her bedchamber. Sliding out of bed, she hobbled to the window, threw the drapes aside and smiled at the morning. It was early, and though there was a light drizzle, the air was warm.

She could hear sounds of activity from downstairs even as delicious aromas wafted up to her. Last night she had eaten so much food that she felt embarrassed. But Abel only smiled indulgently at her, telling her that this was her house now and she could do whatever she wanted.

And speaking of Abel, she couldn't believe that he had come back for her. He was the kindest and most generous man she had ever met. Even though he was now clearly very wealthy, he was still the same humble Abel that she'd grown up with and known. And he loved her; that was clear. When she'd asked him about his supposed marriage to Miss Catherine Landon he'd made things clear to her.

"Miss Catherine Landon was Captain Trent's cousin and she had the mistaken notion that I would make a good husband for her. That was why she went ahead and placed a notice of our supposed engagement in the newspapers. But when that didn't work, she claimed that I had seduced and then ruined her. Thankfully, Captain Trent believed in my innocence, and that was why he sent me back to Europe to get away from her and her plans. I never once gave her any impression that I was romantically interested in her and I hope you believe me, Connie. You're the only woman I have ever loved."

"I was made to believe that you had married Miss Landon."

"So many people wronged you in the past, Connie, and I want you to forgive and forget them. Life is starting anew for both of us and now that I've found you, I'm going to do everything that I can to make sure that you will never cry again. All that I have is now yours, and especially this house, Connie. From now until the breath leaves your body, you'll never again be homeless."

His house had six bedrooms, three on the ground floor and three on the first floor. The house also had an attic, but not like the one she was made to sleep in back in Cambridge. Abel's attic was well lit, and he told her that when they had children, he would turn it into their playroom. What astonished Connie even more was the fact that every bedchamber in the house had its own bathroom and a flushing toilet. She'd only heard of indoor toilets but never seen one.

With so much space in his house Abel had asked Mr. and Mrs. Mather to move in with them so he could take care of them. He was so grateful because they had kept Connie safe in the time she'd been in London. But the elderly couple had humbly declined his offer.

"We have our own home, which is very important to us," Mr. Mather had said. "But thank you so much for your kind and generous offer."

When Robert and Claudia Mather wouldn't move in with them as Abel had requested, he decided he would improve their home. He and the couple were going to Euston Road this morning so they could meet with a contractor who would assess their home and see what improvements could be done.

"There you are," Abel rose to his feet when Connie finally came downstairs. "I know I told you that we would go to Euston Road, but first there is somewhere else I would like us to pass."

"Where is that?" She was feeling a little breathless and knew it wasn't because of the walk from her bedroom. He was the one who had her all flustered. Even though she was here now, it still felt like a dream.

"You'll just have to wait and see, my darling," he said as he crossed the room and led her to the dining table.

"If I continue to eat like this, I won't be able to fit into my new clothes," Connie protested as Abel heaped her plate with bacon, pancakes and beans. She hadn't believed it when, after being shown to the bedchamber, Abel had opened the closet and pointed out the rows of beautiful gowns that were arraigned in it. He had bought them for her even before finding her because he'd told her that he'd been prepared to search for her for the rest of his life.

"You deserve everything good and you look so beautiful today," he admired the plain yellow frock that she was wearing. "And your hair grew back again just as if your mother had never shaved it off. And remind me to give you the wig I had fashioned from the hair you lost four years ago."

They ate in silence for a while; then she smiled sadly.

"What is it?"

"If my mother could see me now," she murmured, remembering all the times that she hadn't been allowed to sit at the dining table with the family.

Abel didn't ever want to see pain and sadness in her eyes, "Remember what I told you, my darling?" she raised her eyes to him, "That no matter how long the night may last, dawn will break and morning will come," he leaned forward, "It is morning for you and I don't ever want you to think about the past or let whatever happened hurt you again."

Connie nodded, "Thank you."

"What are you thinking about now," he asked a few minutes later when he noticed the faraway look in her eyes.

"I can't believe that you're here, and with all this," she waved her hand. "It's just too much for me to take in at once."

"Believe me, I know just what you mean," he grinned. "When my unit was ambushed in India and I was injured, I woke up to find myself in a poor man's home. For some reason Mr. Prakash and his cousin Mr. Samji had been hunting and got caught up in the battle between the British Army and the Indian Rebels. To this day, I'll never know why they chose to save my life and not another soldier's."

Connie reached out a hand and placed it over his and he squeezed it gently. "I'm glad that they saved you for my sake."

"I'm thankful to God for that," his knuckle gently brushed her cheek. "One of the duties allocated to me as part of Mr.

Prakash's family was to hunt for wild hares with his sons. The boys," Connie saw his fond smile, "Anuj and Rakesh loved hunting in the caves and one day they brought back some stones, which I didn't even notice at first. But when I did, I discovered that the boys had found rose quartz, a semi-precious type of gem. Can you believe that for decades and possibly centuries that wealth had lain hidden in those caves just waiting for me," he shook his head. "The first time I sold some of the gems and held money in my hands, I thought I would run mad. It was so much that I was trembling, and it was a good thing that the Indian jeweller was a good man else he would have fleeced me for sure. Then I came back to England and the first thing I wanted to do was to build you a house right here in London, but then buying seemed even better." He looked up at the ceiling and then back at her. "When I saw this house, I knew it was just right for you, for us. My love, before I presume too much, will you be my wife?"

"I'd like nothing more than that."

"Thank you, and I promise that you'll never be sorry. Now finish up your breakfast so we can run a few errands and also take care of Mr. and Mrs. Mather's affairs."

∽

The first place Abel took Connie to was a doctor's office. It was a private practice, and from what she could see, only the wealthy were treated by the physician.

"What are we doing here?" she whispered when they were shown into the doctor's office and asked to sit and wait for him.

"Dr. Donald is one of the best orthopaedic surgeons in England, possibly the world." He looked at her leg, "You will walk again because I am determined that your leg will be properly treated and set."

"But I am all right," Connie knew it would be a very expensive surgery. She could live with the pain now that she had found the love of her life again.

"My darling, you walk with a limp and from time to time I see you groan in pain. You didn't deserve to have your leg broken and I don't want you to continue being in pain. And also, I would like for you to dance at our wedding without feeling any pain."

"But..." before she could say anything else, the doctor opened the door. He was a tall and thin man.

"Sergeant Abel, it's good to see you away from the battlefield. How is Captain Trent doing?"

"I last saw him about two weeks ago and to our delight, he's started walking unaided and has put the crutches away. Right now, he's using a walking stick and getting stronger each day. We are all hopeful that he'll make a full recovery."

"Glad to hear that, now what can I do for you?"

As Abel explained about Connie's injuries, and what he'd done four years ago to set her leg, the doctor asked her to climb onto the examination table.

"It's clear that the bones weren't set right." Dr. Donald said after a thorough examination. "But because you are young, it is a simple procedure. We'll have to break the bones and reset them right this time."

"Break my bones?" Connie turned white when she heard the doctor's words. She couldn't go through that pain again. "No," she looked so horrified and white that Abel thought she would swoon.

"Connie, calm down. It won't be as painful as you imagine it."

"I can't go through that again," Connie shook her head, "The pain nearly killed me the first time. If you hadn't been there, I would have died."

"Miss, if I may?" the doctor's look was sympathetic, "While I admit that there will be some pain, we have made strides in medicine. It will only be for six weeks and then you will have some physiotherapy; soon your leg will be as good as new."

"What if I can't walk again?" she looked down at her leg. "Even though I walk with a limp at least I can still move. I don't want the operation."

The doctor looked at Abel as if seeking further opinion from him.

"Connie," Abel turned to her looking into her eyes. "You don't have to have the operation if you don't want to."

"I don't want it," she whispered. "I can live with a little pain."

"But the longer you live with pain the more it harms your life."

"How?"

Abel turned to the doctor, "Please explain what you told me."

"Miss Connie, the fact that you're in pain means that there are some twisted nerves in your leg. That's not good because that condition will only get worse. You may think that you can live with that pain but if the nerves continue to be twisted it could cause more problems and you could lose your foot."

"What?"

"Yes, Miss Connie, the leg would have to be amputated in the end. So, wouldn't you rather have a little pain and discomfort for say three months and then be well?"

Put like that Connie had no choice but to agree to the operation.

After scheduling the procedure for a week's time, they left the doctor's surgery.

"Connie, you know I love you just the way you are," Abel held her close as the carriage rolled through London. "I wouldn't change a thing about you, but I don't want to see you in pain."

"I know," she whispered, feeling very miserable, "I'm just scared."

"I know but I'll be there with you every step of the way just as I was in that loft four years ago. You will never be alone again to face the pain. And this time everything will be done by proper doctors. It will all turn out right."

"All right," she whispered.

"Now smile for me, my darling," and she did.

∼

Mr. and Mrs. Mather were waiting for them at home. Abel had told them that he never wanted them to go begging again.

"From here and now, I will take care of you just like you took care of my beautiful Connie. And we have more news for you," he explained about the surgery Connie was set to undergo in a week's time. "She will be recuperating for twelve to sixteen weeks and that's how long it will take for your house to be modified. So, if it won't be a problem, would the two of you please come and live with us? In that way I will know that you're being taken care of, and you'll also be good company for Connie. She'll really need you."

"We wouldn't want to impose on your kindness when you're already doing so much for us," Mrs. Mather protested.

"You would actually be doing me a great favour because there is so much I have to do as I set up my business ventures here in London. Also, I will be making one or two trips back to Bombay to see Mr. Prakash and I don't want Connie to be alone at home. With the two of you there, she will be in your good hands and also won't be lonely. But first, I would like you to be our witnesses as we get married because I don't want to wait any more."

Connie frowned slightly, "You want to marry me before the surgery?"

"Yes, and to give you a few days of a good honeymoon before you have to have the surgery. I love you and can't wait to be your husband."

They got married by special licence, and Connie was so happy to finally belong to Abel. On their first night as a married couple, Abel smiled at his wife.

"What is it?" She felt very shy.

"When I first saw you when you were six years old, I told myself that I would one day grow up and marry you. It seems like a very long time ago but I'm so happy that it has finally come to fruition."

"I don't know what to say," she sighed. "It all seems like a dream and I never once imagined that this day would come when we would be together and without anybody threatening us."

"And this is how it will be for the rest of our lives. Now, we have three days to ourselves before your surgery and I want you to put everything out of your mind and let's just enjoy our honeymoon, short as it may be. But I promise that when you are well, we'll have a longer one and I'll even take you to India to meet my friends."

"I'd like that very much."

~

The surgery went well without a hitch and she spent only two days at the private hospital. Even though the place had every luxury that any post-surgery patient could wish for, all she wanted was to go back home and be with her husband. Two days later when she came home, she found that Mr. and Mrs. Mather had moved in. Abel had allocated them one of the downstairs bedchambers so they wouldn't have to use the stairs. Because of the surgery he had also prepared a second room for the two of them, also downstairs.

"This is the advantage of having a big house," he told her as he got her settled in. "We can use whichever bedchamber we want."

"I thought we would use the ones upstairs."

"With time and when you've properly recovered, we'll go back to our bedchamber upstairs. I don't want you straining your leg in any way as you recover; climbing those stairs every day will only cause you to overstrain your leg and impede your recovery."

"You really are spoiling me," Connie was completely sure of her husband's love for her and was growing more confident with each passing day.

"You haven't been spoilt, my lovely Connie. Just wait until I take you to Paris and then New York on one of those new liners. That's when you'll know what being spoilt really is."

But when he left her to go to check up on his business ventures, she felt a little overwhelmed but told herself to stop looking a gift horse in the mouth. She was glad that Abel had convinced her to have the surgery. Now she had just another ten or so weeks of recuperating and physiotherapy. She would get through this, and what made her happy was having Mr. and Mrs. Mather in the house with her.

"A person can get used to all this luxury," Mrs. Mather said as she took a sip of the tea the maid had set out in Connie's chamber. "You are really lucky, child."

Connie winced as she tried to sit up. "I am really happy that you are with me."

She looked up when Abel entered the room and smiled. She loved this man with her whole heart, and his kindness to her and to others was overwhelming.

"I hope you are not straining yourself," he said as he helped her sit with ease. "I know you're eager to get going, but there is no hurry now, is there?"

Connie had a strong reason for wanting to get better quickly. While she knew that Abel loved her, she didn't want to become an unnecessary burden to him. Her one fear was that he might get tired and regret why he had hastened their wedding.

What if he got to a point and felt that she was too much trouble for him? The last thing any man needed or wanted was an invalid for a wife. Now that Abel was very successful and wealthy, there were definitely tons of women more beautiful and healthier than she was. It was just a matter of time before one of them caught his eye and he decided she wasn't what he wanted.

"Right, open your heart and talk to me," Abel entered their bedchamber after dinner that evening. Mr. and Mrs. Mather had already gone to bed and it was because of them that dinner was usually served very early.

"What?" she looked at him, noting the intensity in his eyes.

Their room was well lit with bright gas lamps, and there was no hiding anything from him.

'You've been rather down in spirit and please don't tell me that it's because you are recuperating. Something else is going on with you and I want to hear it."

"I don't know what you mean," her fingers played with the quilt.

"Connie," his voice was quiet but there was firmness too. "I have all night to sit here and wait for you to tell me what is ailing you."

Connie bit her bottom lip, torn between wanting to tell him about her fears and not being willing to make him think that she was just a foolish and emotional woman.

"Connie..."

"I'm not right for you," she finally blurted out, not knowing what else to do. There was a determined look on his face, and she knew that one way or another, he was determined to get answers from her.

"Would you care to explain that statement to me, please?" He sat back on the small couch in their bedroom and folded his arms across his chest.

"Look at me, Abel," tears shimmered in her eyes, "I'm a cripple and not of any use to you. I know that you feel pity for me, but I don't want to you to feel like you owe me anything."

He looked at her for a while then sighed, "Listen to me and listen very well, my little confused darling. I don't pity you but I do have compassion because of the suffering you endured for years. Secondly, you're not a cripple and you are most certainly not useless to me or to anyone else," he rose and moved to sit on the day bed, taking her hands, "Connie I love you so much, you are my life."

"But you didn't have to marry me before you were sure that you wanted to spend the rest of your life with me. I know that the doctor said I would walk again but what if he was wrong?"

Abel touched her cheek, "Connie, I told you that, from when you were six years old, I decided deep in my heart that I would marry you. Nothing has changed from that day, and remember what I told you. I was ready to come and get you back from Mr. Pitcher even if it meant giving up all my wealth. That's how much I love you. A simple crooked leg will not stop me from continuing to show you how much I love you."

∼

It was raining when Mr. and Mrs. Baker and their four children left Malone Manor. To ensure that they left, Mr. Richard Malone had hired some men to stand guard and watch as they exited with only their clothes.

"Where are we supposed to go," Mrs. Baker looked at her husband who sat in a wheelchair and her daughters who were trying to hide their shame under heavy cloaks. "This has been our home for over twelve years."

"You should have thought about how you treated the rightful owner of the place. Because of your wickedness you now find yourselves homeless. Just leave before I make things even worse for you. But to show you that I still have some semblance of humanity in me, I have asked the footman to take you wherever you want to go."

"Won't you give us even a little money to rent a place to live?"

"Mrs. Baker, you're beginning to try my patience. Count all the allowances that Mr. Blackwell gave you for all those years and yet you didn't use the money for its intended purposes. You have jewellery and expensive clothes, which I suggest you sell, and I'm sure that will fetch you a tidy sum that you can use to settle down. This estate will never again support you and your family," and with those words, Mr. Malone entered the house and closed the front door. Mrs. Baker winced when she heard the bolts being put in place, a sure sign that their presence here was no longer welcome.

The Bakers were soon to realise that Ritter's Village was a very small place indeed, and gossip was rife about them and their fall from grace. Everywhere Mrs. Baker went she was met with funny looks and subtle but snide remarks and she started avoiding going to public places. But someone had to earn a living for them, and she found that even servants' positions weren't open for her. She had sold everything that was precious to them, but the money seemed to be falling into a pocket full of holes.

15
DARKNESS HAS PASSED

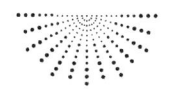

Connie was silent as the carriage rolled down the road toward Justice Lamb's residence. She couldn't help but shudder at the terrible memories of her life in this village.

"Are you cold, my darling?" Abel was concerned at the pinched look around her lips. He noticed also that her knuckles were white, where she gripped her purse. Reaching for the carriage blanket, he placed it over her knees. "Is that better?"

"Yes, thank you, but I wasn't really feeling cold," she whispered huskily.

"Connie, I know this is the last place on earth you want to be, and I promise that as soon as our visit with Justice Lamb and my parents is over, we'll return home to London. I wanted them to share in our happiness."

"I'm sorry to seem so ungrateful for all that you've done for me," she tried to smile but felt the tears instead.

"There's nothing to be sorry for because this place invokes equally terrible memories for me, and its what I call a necessary evil."

"What if they see me?"

Abel knew who "they" were; her family and probably Henry Pitcher's sisters, too. "You left this place a victim but have returned a victor. You left a downtrodden woman but have returned as a conqueror. Yes, I look forward to your family finding out that you have returned. They wanted to destroy your life and did everything possible to expedite you out of this world. But the Lord did not let them overcome you."

Connie listened to Abel, her heart getting stronger. What he said was true, and she knew she had indeed overcome so many obstacles in her life.

"And just know this, even if they show up looking for you, it doesn't mean that you have to speak with them. Captain Trent and his father, the judge, know everything because I told them. We will defend and protect you, and you never have to fear again."

The driver gently brought the horse to a halt and that's when Connie realized that they had arrived at their destination. It was a beautiful manor with lush gardens which were carefully trimmed.

Abel stepped down first, then helped Connie to dismount. He took her by the waist and gently put her on the ground, looking anxiously into her face. "Any discomfort?"

She shook her head, taking a small step and then another. Her leg was completely healed, and she no longer felt any pain when she walked. "As good as new," she grinned up at him, then looked toward the large front door as it opened and three people stepped out, two men and a woman.

"Oh Abel," the woman had a warm and welcoming look on her face as she hurried down the ten steps. "You're back, my son," she hugged him.

"Mrs. Lamb, "Abel hugged her, then gently pulled away, "This is my beautiful wife, Connie. Connie, Mrs. Lamb is the honourable Justice Lamb's wife and Captain Trent's mother. She is like a mother to me."

Connie stretched her hand out to greet the woman but was instead engulfed in a warm embrace that brought tears to her eyes. Her mother had never hugged her, not once, yet this stranger was showing her so much affection.

Once they were inside the house and introductions done, Justice Lamb turned to Abel, "I can't believe that we've been looking all over for Miss Connie and yet she was with you all this time."

Abel saw Connie stiffen as he turned to the judge, "I hope there's no problem."

"No, no," Justice Lamb laughed and leaned forward, "It turns out that there's someone who has been searching for Miss Connie for a long time."

"Who is it?" Abel's voice was sharp.

"Her Uncle Richard."

Connie and Abel looked at each other.

"I don't have any uncle named Richard"

"You wouldn't know him because he's been in America since you were just a few weeks old."

"Is he my mother's brother?"

"No, your father's brother."

"Mr. Gerald's brother?"

"Not Mr. Gerald, Your birth father."

"Is my father still alive then?"

"No, he died twelve years ago when you were six. He left you a large estate and a good inheritance which unfortunately you were never allowed to enjoy."

"I don't understand."

Justice Lamb leaned forward, "According to what your uncle told us, his brother David, your father, wrote to him years ago telling him about you. That was about six months before he died. But your uncle was in America in the West and for seventeen years didn't get any messages from his brother. But a few months ago when he finally returned to New York, a friend told him of your father's death. He didn't stay a day longer in America but took the first ship back, and when he saw Mr. Blackwell, your father's solicitor, he was given letters from his brother that mentioned you. He was happy to have a niece and, according to your father, you were to live on the estate, and Mr. Blackwell was administering your inheritance until you turned twenty-one. Expecting to find you at the estate, your uncle hurried there, only to be informed that you were missing, and your mother and Mr. Gerald had taken over what was rightfully yours."

"Do you mean to say that the estate where Connie grew up actually belonged to her?" Abel's expression was hard.

"Oh yes. Her mother and stepfather moved there when Miss Connie would have been around six years old."

"My mother said one of her wealthy relatives had died and left her an inheritance."

"That was your father, and it was your inheritance, not hers," Justice Lamb chuckled, "The first thing your uncle did when he got here was to get everything in order with your father's solicitor. They had lied to the man that they were taking care of you by presenting one of your sisters. Your uncle threw them out of the estate because they don't belong there. Child, you have your inheritance back."

"I don't want it," Connie shuddered when she thought about the estate where she had been so badly treated. No, she would never set foot in that house again.

"Your Uncle thought you would say that, so he suggested that when he found you, he would ask if he could live there and manage it for you. Of course, all proceeds will go to you since he has made his own wealth."

Connie shook her head, "I don't want to have anything to do with that estate. Let my uncle keep it and give it to anyone he wants, but not me."

"Don't say that, Child. You uncle wants to make amends for his brother's negligence."

Connie didn't want to continue arguing so she fell silent, but deep within her heart she knew that she would never touch anything from that estate.

"Now all we have to do is send a message to your uncle," the judge was saying, and she simply nodded.

∼

"How are you feeling?" Abel asked his wife as he held her in his arms later that night. "Ever since Justice Lamb told you about your uncle, you've been very quiet."

"The day I asked my mother about my father was the day they broke my leg. I had overheard the servants talking about me not being Mr. Gerald's daughter." She remembered the day as if it were just yesterday. "Mary and Anne had messed up the kitchen by spilling milk all over the place and when I asked them why they were being so mean, they told my mother that I had caused the mess." She shook her head. "On top of shaving my head off, she hit me with the pitcher of milk and Mr. Gerald joined in. I was so tired of them treating me badly so when they started hitting me, I told them to take me to my father," she laughed, a sad sound that tore at Abel's heart, "Mr. Gerald told me he was taking me to my father, and that meant that he would kill me so I would join my father in the other world."

"I'm so sorry, Connie."

"I know that Mr. Gerald wasn't my father and so he thought he could treat me however he wanted, but my own mother," she wept softly, "Why would my own mother have hated me so much that she treated me so badly and allowed Mr. Gerald to do the same?"

"One day she will answer for her crimes but for now I don't want you to ever worry about anything. The judge said your uncle will be coming to see you tomorrow. At least listen to what he has to say before completely shutting him out."

∽

Uncle Richard turned out to be a handsome man who didn't waste any time but hugged Connie.

"You could be my daughter," he said with tears in his eyes as he held her close. "I'm so sorry that we are meeting after so many years," He held her by the shoulders, "Your husband's parents told me about the pain and anguish you've lived with all these years under the care of those ingrates."

"Why didn't my father take me away from my mother even before he died?" Tears coursed down her face, "Didn't he want me at all? What can his inheritance do for me after all that I have suffered?"

"Connie," Richard sighed, leading her to the couch even as Abel hovered. "My brother made a lot of mistakes in his lifetime. He and his wife couldn't have children and that created a lot of problems in their marriage. That was the reason he got into a relationship with your mother who was a maid on the estate. When she told David that she was expecting you, his wife somehow found out and threw her off the estate."

Connie felt something like pity for her mother. It couldn't have been easy for her as a young woman, pregnant and without a home. Maybe that was the reason she had hated Connie.

"Was that why she hated me so much?" Connie asked.

"When my brother found out that his wife had sent Dinah away, he looked for her and offered to support her and her baby. He even brought both of you back to the estate. But his wife died a month or so after your mother put to bed, and she got married to Mr. Gerald Baker. But they worked something out, so he supported her to take care of you. The agreement was that when you turned two years, she would take you to him."

"Why didn't she take me to my father then?"

"Because she was greedy and wanted more. I found an old servant who told me that Dinah would bring you to see your father and she would just demand more money. Each time he asked her to leave you with him, she threatened to expose him," Richard chuckled, "My brother was a man who cared about what people said about him. The thought of a maid exposing him for having sired her child gave him nightmares. For six years, your mother milked my brother for what he could give her. When he died, he left everything to you and that was when your mother took over your inheritance."

Richard took his niece's hand, "You paid a high price for your parents' mistakes but not anymore. For as long as I live, no one will ever hurt you again," he looked at Abel, "And that goes for you too, Mr. Abel. My niece is in your hands now, and I expect you to cherish and treat her well. Or else you'll have to answer to me."

"Yes, Sir,"

"Good. Now, what would you like to do with your property?"

"I understand you sent my mother out of the estate."

"Yes, I did, and I had some pretty nasty word exchanges with your father's solicitor for not doing a better job of monitoring your progress through the years, though it really wasn't his fault. The man suffered a stroke, but mercifully he has recovered. But while he was indisposed, his son who is a junior partner in his firm was overseeing things, and your mother, that crafty woman, found a way of exacting money from what your father left you. He has been reprimanded and everything has been sorted out. In his time, your father made some good investments so even if your mother wasted much over the years, there's still something for you to inherit."

"I don't want that house or anything from that estate."

"And I understand," he gently rubbed the back of her hand with his thumb. "The old servant I mentioned before told me all about the abuse and mistreatment at your mother's and stepfather's hands. That was the reason I actually threw them off the estate. Had they treated you right, I would have let them continue staying there."

"So what happens now?"

"Since I'm back in England, I was thinking of buying some property. But if you will allow me, I can take over the estate and run it. And all proceeds will go to you."

Connie shook her head, "I don't want anything from that estate. My father should have tried harder to take me away from my mother."

"Well, then I'll put all the money into a trust fund for your children. Let them have what you didn't, and that is what my brother would have wanted, too."

"But…"

"Connie," Abel called out, "Your father lost the chance to have his daughter and bring her up. He was wrong not to fight for you, but he did his best and your mother is not an easy woman to handle."

Her husband's words made sense and she mellowed, but only slightly.

∼

Grant and John came running and burst into the house, their eyes wide with terror, and they ran and hid under the rickety bed.

"What is going on?" Mary asked them as she shifted to find a more comfortable position on the floor where she was sitting. Anne was sleeping on the mat, and their mother was preparing some oatmeal over the fire in the small hearth. Their father was pretending to doze in his wheelchair.

There was a loud pounding on the door. "Open up in the name of the law," a harsh voice said, and they all started. "Open up before we break this door down."

"Mary, open the door."

"No Mama, I'm afraid to."

Mrs. Dinah Baker looked at her daughter with annoyance then went to open the door. It was the village constable, and he didn't look too happy. "Sir, is there a problem?"

"Where are your two sons?"

"Have they done anything wrong?"

"Those boys have been picking people's pockets and were warned before. But I'm done looking the other way even if you are having troubles, Lady. I have come to arrest them."

"Constable," Mrs. Baker looked at her family then stepped out of the house and closed the door. "I'll do anything, please don't arrest my sons. They are just little boys."

"Your sons are fifteen and fourteen years old, and I'm running out of patience with them. There's only so much I can do to protect them and you."

"I am really sorry," Mrs. Baker looked around to make sure no one was watching, then she drew closer to him. "I will make it up to you, but you know that we are really going through a very tough time."

"Well, just be warned that this is the last time I am looking the other way. Besides, why don't you go and ask your daughter to help you now that she is a wealthy woman."

"My daughters are with me and we are doing poorly."

The constable made an impatient sound, "I'm not talking about those two; I mean your oldest daughter, the one who was once supposed to have been married to Mr. Henry Pitcher," he shook his head. "I never understood how a small girl like that would get married to a man nearly three times older than her own father, but well, seeing your other two and now that they are in the family way, it tells me a lot. You should have found them old and wealthy men to marry them," he chuckled at his own joke. "Then they wouldn't have brought you the shame of being unwed mothers. But now you can go and ask your daughter to give you some money to live on. She returned from London with her very wealthy husband and they are staying at Justice Lamb's place. Surely a girl won't turn her own mother away."

And the constable left, not knowing he had left a very frightened woman behind.

16

THE MORNING COMES

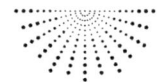

The next morning as Connie sat in the small, brightly lit parlour of Judge Lamb's house, she allowed her thoughts to go slowly back over the events of the past few years. Her mind remembered every single word of abuse, and her body tensed at every blow that she had received.

She didn't know that she was crying until her husband crouched before her and wiped her tears away.

"You promised that you wouldn't think about the things that made you sad."

"I'm sorry," she looked down.

"Oh, my darling, "Abel sat next to her and pulled her into his arms, "You are safe now, and no one will ever come near you to harm you."

"I can't help thinking about my mother and wondering why she hated me so much," Connie wept, "She should have just left me with my father."

"I don't have an answer for that, my love, but all I can tell you is that you are loved. You have a new family in your uncle Richard, the judge and Mrs. Lamb, Captain Trent and his fiancée and me. We love you so much and will always be here for you. We are your family."

They heard the doorbell ringing and then a few minutes later, one of the maids came into the parlour.

"Sir, there is a man in a wheelchair and a woman and four youngsters at the door."

"What do they want? Mrs. Lamb isn't here to deal with charity cases. Give them some food and then ask them to come back later." Captain Trent's mother ran a charity that provided food and clothing for the less privileged in life.

The maid hesitated, nervously fingering her apron.

"Naomi, what is it?"

"Sir, they asked for Mrs. Connie."

Abel's eyes narrowed as he rose to his feet, "No," he told his wife who had started rising, "You stay here, and I'll get to the bottom of this. We don't know who is standing out there and the last thing I want is for any harm to come to you."

Abel headed toward the front door, but Justice Lamb and Uncle Richard beat him to it.

"What do you want," Abel heard Richard's shout before he saw who the visitors were.

"I have a right to see my daughter," Mrs. Dinah Baker said haughtily, "I was told that she is here, and I want to see her."

"What right?" Richard looked so imposing and Abel saw Mrs. Baker turn very pale. "Woman, I was the one who set this trap so you could all show up here, and I was right. Just the

179

right words in the village constable's ears and here you are. You're nothing but a greedy and avaricious opportunist and let me get this clear to you, Connie is my niece, my brother's daughter who you abused for years. My biggest regret is that I was not in touch with my brother and it was because of you, Dinah. When I realized that my brother was being unfaithful to his wife with you, we had a terrible row and I left home. But he also found out what kind of a woman you were, and that was why his will was iron clad. You weren't worthy of inheriting anything from him, and that was why he left it all for his daughter. But you weren't content to enjoy the privileges offered by the estate; you wanted it all for yourself. Now as you can see, you've lost it all."

Connie had moved from the inner parlour to the living room because she wanted to hear everything that was being said. But the one thing she had no desire of doing was seeing her mother, stepfather and siblings. The pain and anguish returned, and it took all her strength not to burst out on the porch and scream for them to leave and never come back again.

"My brother left his wealth to his only daughter. If you had been a good mother, you would have taken good care of Connie. She was the goose that was to lay golden eggs for you if I may put it like that, but you couldn't even be kind to her," Richard turned his eyes to Gerald who was in a wheelchair. "And you," he pointed at the man who practically squirmed, "You attacked my niece when she asked about her father, breaking her leg and crippling her. As if that was not enough, you tried to force yourself on her. But for Abel's intervention, only God knows what harm you would have done to my innocent niece." His eyes went back to Mrs. Baker, "Your own daughter, you said, yet you allowed your worthless husband to attack her. And then instead of even defending your daughter, you sold her off to a man three times her age."

There was silence and Connie wanted to hear what her mother's defence would be, but she remained silent.

Uncle Richard went on, "Abel was to have been hanged or imprisoned, but for Justice Lamb's intervention. And all because he was defending an innocent young woman from your wicked husband. Now tell me, what is your defence? My brother may have been a weak man, but you are now dealing with me, and woman, I know your kind. I discovered that you and Henry had an affair, and that was why he blackmailed you into selling your own daughter to him."

Connie slumped in her seat, covering her face. She couldn't believe how wicked her own mother had been.

"That's a lie," Mrs. Baker blurted out, "He was a liar and a good-for-nothing."

"And yet that was the man you sold your daughter to. But it wasn't Henry who told me about your trysts. His sisters knew and what's more, there's much doubt about your two last children's parentage."

"No," Dinah moaned, turning to Gerald, her eyes wild, "They are your children. Don't listen to this bitter man."

"Bitter?" Richard threw his head back and laughed, "Woman, I am not bitter, I am very angry, and you should be glad that the judge, the Captain and Abel are here. I've lived in the American Wild West and believe me, I'm not a man you want to cross. I brought you here because I wanted to make it clear to you that you will never set eyes on Connie ever again."

"I'm her mother."

"You should have behaved like her mother these past eighteen years. She was the means to your good life but never again."

"Connie has a good heart and she will want to see me," Dinah insisted, "Connie, come out here my dear, it's your mother."

Though Connie knew her mother couldn't see her, she still shrank back in the seat, trembling. Abel knew that Connie would have heard her mother's voice and went back inside. He found her shaking on the couch and was immediately at her side.

"My darling, she can never hurt you again."

"Why did they come here?"

"Your uncle was the one who made them come. I think he wants you to have closure so that you can never be afraid of them again."

"I don't ever want to see them again," and the deep sobs that wrecked her body were nearly his undoing. He held her close and allowed her to cry until she was spent.

"No one can ever make you see those people. But all we want is for you to face them and see that they no longer have any power over you."

Connie thought about what Abel was saying and nodded slightly, "Do I have to speak with them?"

"Not if you don't want to. I want you to see how weak they are and let them go. Get them out of your mind and your heart. The picture you have of them in your mind is of them being imposing and strong. Yet they are only human and weak and that was why they allowed wickedness to rule them. Strong people like Justice Lamb and his family are kind and compassionate. Weak people are insecure and wicked. Fear doesn't have to rule you for the rest of your life, my Love. You now have a family and people who love you so much, and we will make sure that no one can ever hurt you again."

"I just feel so much pain when I think that Mr. Pitcher could have harmed me, and Mr. Gerald too, yet my own mother let it happen."

"God protected you and their evil schemes came to naught. Never again will you be in the power of such wicked people. You're a very strong woman who has been through terrible ordeals and emerged as a victor. Don't let the past rob you of a bright future."

Connie thought for a while. Just two days before, Mrs. Lamb had found her crying in the garden and sat beside her not saying a word at first.

"I feel your pain," she had finally said, "When those who should have taken care of you, protected you and been there for you hurt you instead, it wounded your heart. But child, you can't continue to live with so much pain because you will one day turn on Abel and really hurt him."

"No," Connie wiped her tears, "I could never hurt Abel, I love him so much and he's been nothing but good to me since I was a child."

"Not willingly and knowingly, you wouldn't hurt him. But pain that is not dealt with and put away festers into bitterness and before you know it, a good man will begin to pay for the sins of the wicked. Don't allow or make Abel be the recipient of your bitterness when he doesn't deserve it."

"But what do I do?"

"Forgive all who have wronged you."

"They never said sorry, not even once did they acknowledge that what they were doing to me was wrong," she responded angrily. "They tormented me, crippled me and did terrible things to me. Why should I forgive them?"

"Because the Bible compels us to forgive those who have trespassed against us as our Father in heaven has also forgiven us. And it doesn't matter if they will ever ask for forgiveness or not. If you hold onto unforgiveness then they continue to chain and enslave you."

"I don't know if I can do that."

"All I ask is that you think about it. The more you don't forgive the more you are forced to revisit the pain inflicted on you, and the more bitter you get. Soon thoughts of revenge take over and that is when you will begin to lash out at even those who love you." Mrs. Lamb rose to her feet and gently patted Connie's shoulder. "Think about it."

And now as she heard her mother's voice coming from outside, she realized what she must do.

"I think I'm ready to face them," she rose to her feet and Abel smiled at her. "But I can't do this alone."

"And you will never have to do it alone, ever again. The judge and his wife as well as Uncle Richard are all out there. Ready now?" she nodded and with his arms around her, they walked out of the door and stepped onto the porch.

"See," Dinah pointed triumphantly, "I told you my Connie would want to see me."

When Uncle Richard would have spoken, Connie shook her head. She was trembling inwardly, but her face was calm as she faced the people who had made her life hell.

"Mother, Mr. Gerald, Anne, Mary, Grant, John, I forgive you," she said in a clear and loud voice. "I also ask for your forgiveness because I wasn't the daughter or sister that you deserved. Please forgive me."

Connie saw her mother's face crumple, and her stepfather turned white, swallowing repeatedly. As for her siblings, they couldn't even look at her.

"My work here is done," she told Abel and saw not only love but deep respect in his eyes.

"Wait," her mother called out, holding her hand out, "Come back home, Connie. We can be a family again," she looked at Gerald who nodded, "Let's forget the past and I promise you that this time things will be better."

"Mother. I have chosen to forgive you and Mr. Gerald and even my siblings. But that doesn't mean that I can ever trust you again. So, no thank you," she smiled at her uncle, the judge, his wife, Captain Trent and Abel. "I have a new family now and they love me unconditionally. Good-bye, mother," and saying this, she went back into the house, her heart feeling free, and she knew that she would be all right.

Richard, however, wasn't done with the unwanted visitors. "My niece is a very gentle-hearted child who was taken advantage of by all of you. Me, however, I am not so forgiving. So, this is what will happen. You will leave this place and never return."

"But where will we go? We have nothing left," Mrs. Baker begged, "If you would just allow us back home."

Richard cut her off, "Which home? That is my niece's property, and you will never set foot on it again. No, I would have tossed all of you in prison, but since I know that will hurt my niece, I won't. Instead, I am going to get you as far away from Connie as possible. I even have a mind to take you all the way to America and dump you in the wilderness."

"No," they were all trembling.

"But for the sake of the niece I love, I won't send you out of England. But I will send you to the furthest corner of North England. So, here is what will happen. Today, you will rest in the inn close to the railway station and first thing tomorrow, I'll put you on a train to Wigton."

"Wigton?" Anne shrieked, "Where is that?"

"You'll find out when you get there and if any of you tries to run away, the arrangement is off, and I will hunt you down like I hunted bison in America. You can never hide from me. And when I find you, it will be prison where you will all pay for your crimes and the judge here will back me up. There's enough evidence to put you all away for a very long time."

'Connie can't do this to us," Mary said, "Mother, beg her to let us stay."

"Connie has nothing to do with this," Abel spoke for the first time, "I am her husband and will do everything I can to keep her safe."

"She's our sister," Grant said.

"You should have remembered that all those times you insulted. It made you happy to see her suffer, but never again," Abel shook his head. "Do you remember what I told you many years ago, that when you do good then you will reap good, but wickedness begets wickedness and that's what is happening to all of you now."

"If you don't want to go to Wigton that is fine," Richard said and the six smiled, "But you are going straight to jail." Their faces paled. "You have five minutes to decide, after which the offer is withdrawn."

"But what will we do in Wigton?" Mrs. Baker asked resignedly.

"Funny that you should ask," Richard was clearly enjoying himself. "My good friends, Lord and Lady Ainsworth own a penal house in Wigton and you will all work there as servants, even Gerald in your wheelchair. See how it feels when the shoe is on the other foot and you are forced to bear the brunt of other people's ill treatment. And don't for one moment imagine life will be easy. Lord Ainsworth is a man who does not suffer fools gladly."

17
THE EVILS THAT MEN DO

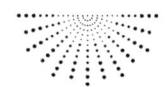

"What I don't understand is how a woman who looks so genteel as you, Mrs. Baker, can be so wicked, "Mrs. Lamb said, "Women are always thought of as caring mothers, protectors and nurturers. But you, Mrs. Dinah, did everything in your power to destroy your own child's life. What mother is so mean to her own child in such a horrible way?"

"A mother who never gave birth to the child in the first place," a voice spoke up and they all turned to see who the newcomer was. A couple had suddenly appeared from behind the main house.

Abel was watching Mrs. Baker's face, and he saw her turning as white as a ghost.

"Veronica?" she looked like she was choking.

The stranger stepped forward and pulled the scarf off her head and everyone gasped. One side of her face was badly burnt.

"My name is Veronica and Dinah here is my younger sister," she had tears in her eyes. "She is a wicked and vicious woman who wanted me dead so she could take away everything I had."

"Miss Veronica," Richard stepped forward, "Would you like to sit down?" The woman looked weak and frail. She shook her head and leaned closer to the man she was with.

"This is Jeremiah Blake, my husband," she smiled at Richard, "He is Mrs. Ingrid Malone's brother, Mr. David Malone's brother in law."

"There's a lot of explaining to be done here," Jeremiah's voice was soft but the look he gave was full of love.

"Veronica, I'm sorry" Dinah stuttered.

"No Dinah, you're not sorry about the hell you put me through. You're just sorry that everyone is about to find out just how wicked you are."

"Please…" but everyone ignored her, their eyes on Veronica.

"Jeremiah and I were so much in love and we even got married. The day that I found out that I was pregnant, Dinah, who worked for Jeremiah's sister, came home and told us that she too was pregnant with Mr. David's child." Veronica wiped her tears. "She was a maid in that house and had seduced him because he was wealthy, and his wife couldn't have any children. But she told Jeremiah's sister, Mrs. Rhonda, that I was the one who was pregnant for David."

Everyone gasped as Jeremiah nodded.

"My sister and Mrs. Ingrid then planned on how they would get rid of me. I didn't know why my own sister would plan such evil against me. Unfortunately, at the time, Mr. David was in Europe so he couldn't tell his wife that I wasn't his lover but Dinah was," Veronica shook her head. "We put to bed on the same day, but Dinah's child died. She had spread such malicious rumours about me that people believed her." Veronica wiped her face. "Even Jeremiah briefly thought that I had been unfaithful to him because Dinah put her dead daughter next to me, a child who looked like David. And she took my baby. One month later, Mrs. Ingrid died, and Dinah told everyone that I had poisoned her because I wanted Mr. Malone for myself. I was sentenced to be hanged. This was however changed to transportation to Australia for twenty years."

Dinah crumpled to the ground.

"Dinah thought I was dead, and when Mr. Malone returned, she presented my little baby as the child she had borne for him."

"Now we all understand why this poor child suffered at the hands of this wicked woman," Richard Malone glared at Mrs. Baker, then pointed at her daughters, "Evil returns to reward those who do it. Look at your daughters, Mrs. Baker. They are just sixteen and seventeen and unmarried, yet they will soon be mothers," The two girls gasped, hiding their faces. "And your sons are being sought by the police because someone said they were turning into pickpockets. With your wickedness you sought to destroy other people's lives but see where that has got you."

"Mrs. Veronica, would you please tell us how you managed to get free and come back here?" the judge asked.

"After Dinah accused me of poisoning Mrs. Ingrid and I was arrested, she paid some people to burn the cell where I was being held. I woke up when my cell was engulfed in flames and I was on fire. The prison warden got me out of there, and even though I was badly burned, they still put me on a ship to Australia." Abel saw Jeremiah's arms tighten around his wife. "Jeremiah had believed Dinah's story that I had been unfaithful to him, so he decided to leave for America. But he found out that I was innocent and followed me to Australia, and that's where we've been for the past nearly eighteen years. I was lucky that the employer of the colony where I was dispatched was kind enough to allow Jeremiah to be there with me as I worked out my sentence. Then two years ago, Jeremiah decided to return to England and that's when he decided to do some investigations and to see if we could find our child," she looked at Dinah. "He found out the truth and realized that for eighteen years you had tormented our child, and Jeremiah was even told that she had died. Where is my daughter, Dinah?"

Connie who had heard all the new commotion slowly emerged from the house.

"Jeremiah, she looks just like your mother." Veronica whispered, holding onto her husband as she pointed at Connie.

"Is it true?" Connie whispered to Uncle Richard.

"What they are saying sounds like the truth. I recall hearing some scandal attached to Dinah's sister but at the time I was also dealing with my sister-in-law's illness before she died. We had no idea that she had been poisoned. My brother returned from Europe and everything became a mess after that and I had to leave so yes, what Mrs. Veronica says must be true," he turned to Dinah, "Speak up or it's Australia for you. Now!" His hard tone shook Dinah.

"It is true I exchanged my dead baby for my sister's."

"You will never know peace in your life, Dinah. I pity you because your wickedness has followed you and wreaked havoc on your family."

Connie, held by Abel, slowly walked down the steps until she was standing before her mother and father.

"You are so beautiful," Jeremiah's voice cracked, and then the three of them were in each other's

arms, weeping for all the pain and separation of eighteen years.

∼

"This is a prison," Dinah said in a small voice when the large metal gates were shut with a clang causing them to all wince. "Will we ever leave this place?"

Her two daughters and one son and husband could only look around, saying nothing. They hadn't believed it when Connie pleaded for John not to be exiled with the rest of them.

"He was kind to me and when I was in Mr. Pitcher's house, he used to come and comfort me," she had told everyone. "He's my small brother and I don't want his life to end badly. His heart is still tender enough for him to be shaped into someone good."

And John had stayed behind while the rest of them were put on a train with guards and brought to Wigton. The house was imposing and looked more like a prison than a home.

"This is where you will live out the rest of your lives," a balding man appeared as if from nowhere. "Now come, and I will allocate each of you to your rooms and duties. The penalty for trying to run away is death. The penalty for causing any kind of trouble is death. The penalty for any kind of offence that doesn't warrant death is flogging, and that is twenty-one strokes. Talk back at me or refuse to work and you'll be flogged."

Mary turned to her mother, a very ugly expression on her face, "It's a good thing we are to be separated because for as long as I live, I never want to see you again. You should have taught us better how to be decent human beings, for then this would not have happened to us," she touched her stomach which was big with child. "I have realized my mistakes and sins and for as long as I live, I will make restitution and I will teach my child the right values in life."

"Me too," Anne said with tears in her eyes. "John is so lucky that he changed his heart, and now he will have a good life while the rest of us will die in this place. But I just pray that one day Connie will forgive us."

"Mary, Anne…" Dinah saw the anger and disgust on her family's faces, and she knew that she was paying for her crimes, would continue to pay until the day she died.

18
DEEP CONSIDERATIONS

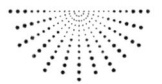

Abel rolled over in bed and realised that he was alone, and from the coolness of the sheets, it seemed he had been that way for a while. He squinted at the bracket clock in the dim light, noticing that it was a little after one o'clock in the morning. He didn't hear any movement in the inner chamber room next door, and he frowned. Where could his wife be at this hour?

"Connie?" He got out of bed and winced when his feet touched the cold floor; then he remembered that the thick carpet that would normally be on the floor had been taken out because it caused his wife to sneeze. In her current condition she was very sensitive, and he wanted to make life as comfortable for her as possible. The fire in the hearth was still burning but he added some wood on it for good measure. It was approaching winter and the nights got very cold.

Hopping from foot to foot, he found his bedroom slippers and sighed when his feet immediately got warm again. Tying the thick robe around himself, he went in search of his wife.

He found her seated in the small private parlour staring unseeingly at the lamp.

"Connie?" He tried to be as soft as possible so as not to startle her and he had to call her three times before she blinked rapidly and turned to look at him.

"I didn't mean to wake you up, sorry about that," she gave him a watery smile and he frowned. Something was wrong, and he rushed to her side, sitting down on the chaise longue with her.

"My love, you look so troubled. You know that I hate seeing you like this. What ails you?"

Connie turned tearful eyes to her husband. He was surprised that there was a plea in them.

"Connie, you know that I would do anything for you and if it were possible for me to capture the sun, the moon and the stars in my hands and give them to you, I would do so in a heartbeat."

"I know that," her voice broke, and Abel was greatly concerned. He had prayed to never see such distress on the face of the woman he loved with his whole heart. She had been through so much all her life and after marrying her he had made a promise to make her happy for the rest of his life. Seeing her like this greatly distressed him but he didn't want her to see that he was thus affected.

"My dearest heart," he placed a hand over her stomach. "You're carrying our first child, and I don't want you to be worried or anxious about anything. Now, please tell me what has caused you so much distress that you're unable to sleep."

"I..." she bit her lower lip nervously. "I don't know how to tell you this."

"You know that you can tell me anything."

"It's about Mary, Anne and Grant," Connie finally got out and saw his countenance change. "Please don't be like that," she pleaded.

"Connie you know that I can do anything for you including walking on hot coals, but when it comes to those people you know what my stand is."

"My darling, please hear me out."

A door opened somewhere in the house and they knew that it was John. A few minutes later, he entered the parlour and came and stood right in front of her, peering into her face.

"Are you all right, Connie?" He looked at her with concern in his eyes. Connie wondered that her youngest brother who was only thirteen had such a mature disposition. "Do you need anything?"

She shook her head and smiled at him. "I was just feeling a little restless because of the heat in our bedchamber but I'm all right."

"I heard voices and got worried about you."

"John, please go to sleep now."

"If you're sure that you're all right."

"Yes, we are," Connie gave him a broad smile. "If anyone is peeping into our house right now, they will wonder that its inhabitants are awake at this ungodly hour."

"Someone will even venture to think that we're having a night feast," Abel said dryly, and Connie giggled.

"I was actually thinking about getting some biscuits and milk but felt too lazy to get to the kitchen."

"I can get them for you," John said hurriedly and before Connie could protest, he was out of the room.

"I'm worried about him," Connie told her husband.

"Why?"

"A young boy like John should be in bed and fast asleep by now. Yet here he is, staying awake with the rest of us. It makes me wonder that he is also anxious and unable to sleep."

"He could just be restless too."

Connie shook her head. "I know he worries about his parents and siblings. John may put on a stoic face, but inside he is just a frightened little boy. Suddenly his whole family was ripped away from him, and apart from knowing that they were in prison he has no idea if they are still alive."

"You're all the family John needs right now."

"No, my little brother is anxious and I'm afraid that it may affect his life in future."

"He knows what those people did and so I don't think he worries about them."

"That's where you're wrong. I was speaking with Miss Fonder his governess, and she mentioned that he always asks her how far Wigton is from this place. Had he asked once or twice, I would have thought nothing of it. But when he started asking about the trains that go up north, it concerned me as it did her, and that was why she decided to let me know what is going on."

Abel looked at her in alarm. "That doesn't sound very good."

Connie nodded, "Abel my love, what if John is planning on running away to go to Wigton? He's just a little boy and there are a lot of dangers lurking out there. It would break my heart if something happened to him."

They heard footsteps and fell silent as John walked in carrying a tray on which was a jug of milk and some cookies on a plate as well as three cups. "Now that we're all up why don't we just indulge in milk and biscuits?" He placed the tray on the table and poured out the milk, handing out the cups and then sitting down on Connie's other side. She always smiled when he sat close to her, even if there were other chairs in a room. She knew that it was his way of wanting to be close to her after he had lost his parents and other siblings and she felt very close to him.

"Did you leave the kitchen in its usual spotless way?"

John grinned at her, "I was very careful because the last thing I want is to bring down the wrath of Cook on my head."

"Very well, let's indulge and then go back to sleep," Connie said. She gave her husband a look that said their discussion was far from over.

∽

Connie revisited their previous conversation when it was light. Being a Saturday morning and given that they had stayed up until nearly three, Abel didn't get up as early as usual.

"I feel guilty for keeping you up all night when you were so tired."

"Connie, your happiness is my priority, and I'm glad that you at least got some rest."

"We didn't finish our conversation because of John."

He sat up and leaned against the headboard. "Are we back to that again?"

"I can't put it out of my mind."

Abel sighed. He could never deny his wife anything. "I'll listen but don't expect me to like what you have to say."

"The fact that you're giving me your ear is good enough for me," she twisted her fingers in her hands. "I know that you don't like hearing anything to do with my family because of how they treated me for so many years."

"That's putting it mildly," he said, and Connie was glad that Abel was on her side. Her husband could be daunting when he wanted to be. "With them banished to Wigton, I never thought I would hear about them ever again, and believe me, I have never lost any sleep over that fact."

"Abel please..."

"I'm listening, though I told you that I might not like what you have to say about those people."

"My mother..."

"That woman is not your mother," Abel growled.

"Very well then," if the matter wasn't very serious, Connie would have giggled at the expression on her husband's face. It was clear that he would never speak of Mrs. Baker without looking like someone who had just taken vinegar. "Mrs. Baker and her husband deserve all the punishment they got because of what they did to me. But Mary, Anne and Grant are paying for crimes they didn't commit, at least not directly. I admit they were often mean to me but banishing them for the rest of their lives is like a death sentence, for they will never be free again. My worry is that Mary and Anne who are about to put to bed will have to bring their little babies up in prison. Isn't that also relegating the next generation into servitude and yet they are innocent children?"

Abel took one of her hands, "Connie, the love of my life, I hear what you're saying but don't you remember the Word that says the sins of the fathers will be visited on the children?"

"It shouldn't be like that because there is also the grace of forgiveness, Abel. The same Word that speaks of the sins of the fathers also mentions in another place that the Lord will not make the children pay for the sins of their fathers. There is grace and forgiveness, or else how will we live in this world?'

Abel's scowl deepened, and Connie touched his face gently.

"Please don't be angry with me for bringing this up because I can see that my words have displeased you."

Abel took a long while before responding; then he sighed and pulled Connie close to him. "This is a very strange conversation that we're having this early morning. Right now, I am feeling angry and don't want to give you any response based on my feelings. But I promise you that I will think about what you've told me, and then I will let you know what I intend to do about everything."

She gave him a smile that melted his insides and snuggled closer to him.

"That's all I ask, dear husband."

19
TIME OF GRACE

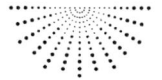

Abel sat in deep thought in his office later that morning, trying to understand his wife's words. He felt that if he didn't handle this situation properly it could create a lot of problems in future, especially for Connie. She was worried about John and with good reason, too. Now that he thought about it, he realised she was right. John was just a young boy whose whole life had been turned upside down, and if they were to make a good man out of him yet, they had to also address all his secret concerns.

"Have you had a look at these invoices...." Trent's voice trailed away when he saw the look on Abel's face. "Has something happened at home to Connie or John?"

Abel shook his head and looked up at his best friend and partner in business. "Connie brought up something early this morning and I don't know how to deal with it."

"Would you care to share?" Trent made himself comfortable in the seat in front of Abel's desk, placing the folder of documents between them.

"My wife hasn't been at peace for a while now, but I had no idea until this morning. At one in the morning she was sitting in the parlour, looking really sad. Then I found out that John has been asking his governess for directions to Wigton."

Trent looked shocked, "You know what that means."

Abel nodded, "And Connie is really worried that he'll decide to run away and go up north to find his family. And she had some very deep things to say about her sisters and brother who are up there." And he shared the conversation he'd had with his wife. "What do you think I should do? If I don't handle this issue with prudence and wisdom it could create a lot of trouble for us in future. The last thing I want is for those people to come anywhere near Connie. They set out to destroy her life, and if I allow them to get close again, who knows what they could be planning? But then again if I sit back and remain firm and do nothing, John could run away and if something happens to him, my wife would never forgive herself." He looked at his friend. "Trent, if it were you, what would you do?"

Trent bent his head for a brief moment then looked up again. "Your wife's anxieties are real, and you should be worried too."

"Why?'

"As you say, all of this has to be handled with a lot of wisdom. The fear is that if your wife's siblings remain behind bars, they could become bitter and vengeful. And who knows, John may find a way of getting to them and seeing their suffering, and that could adversely affect him into seeking retribution for them."

"How then do I work this out so that everyone is at peace with the decision I make?"

"Connie is right when she talks about her siblings not having to pay for the sins of their parents. When it comes to Mr. and Mrs. Baker, I would wish that someone would lock them in a prison underground and throw the key away. But the children only behaved as they were taught. Train up a child in the way he should go, says the good Book. If we train children to love and care for others, then that is how they will be. But if we teach them to hate and discriminate against others then that is what they will do. Those three children were only doing what they were taught to do, but they are still young and can be helped to live better lives. However, that won't happen if they continue to remain in exile, so to speak."

"So would you suggest that I seek to have them freed and bring them to live with us?"

"Not at all. There are consequences to actions and being young isn't an excuse for continued bad behaviour. My suggestion is that you find out if there is any remorse in the hearts of those three children. If there is then it means that whatever was lost can be salvaged."

"How do I do that and yet they are all the way up there?"

"The house has a keeper, and from what I learnt from Mr. Richard, the man is very strict but fair. You could find out from him if there is any change in the lives of those three and then see what you can do after that."

Abel smiled for the first time that morning. "Thank you for that good advice. Believe me, I was really getting anxious about how to handle this whole situation."

The letter arrived one week after Connie and Abel had had their long talk.

"Dear Mr. Pierson,

I received your letter inquiring about the conduct of Miss Mary Baker, Miss Anne Baker and Master Grant Baker and this is what I have to report to you. The three children have surprised all of us here and we were even thinking about writing to ask you to consider leniency on their sentence. While I know that it has only been a short time since they were brought here, there have been vast changes in their characters and dispositions.

For one, the three children are very hard working and never complain. At first, I thought it was because they were afraid since the penalties for disobedience set out for them were very stiff. However, it has come to my attention and that of my other colleagues that all these children needed was a better guiding hand and hope for the future. That being said, your letter couldn't have arrived at a more appropriate time.

To err is human but forgiveness is divine, and your attitude gives me hope that you're not only just thinking about punishment so these children can pay for their ills, but restitution also resounded in your words.

I will be looking forward to receiving your instructions on what else to do with these young ones.

Thank you.

Yours sincerely,

Bernard Miles

Keeper of the House."

∽

Mary, Anne and Grant Baker were cleaning the kitchen and singing softly when they were summoned to the castle keeper's office. They hadn't ever been summoned here because they were determined to stay out of trouble.

"Please sit down," the man spoke politely to them and they were surprised. They hadn't seen him since that day nearly two months ago when he'd received them from their guarded escort and told them all the penalties of bad behaviour. So they looked at each other. Mr. Miles smiled at them. "Please sit down," he leaned forward in his seat and waited until the three were seated. "I know that the first time we met it was under different circumstance. But I've been receiving reports about you for the past two months." The siblings all paled. "No, have no fear, all I've heard is that you are doing very well and there have been no complaints from you or about you."

Mary was the one who spoke for all of them. "Our behaviour in the past was abominable and we know that we're only receiving what is just punishment for our wrong doings."

Mr. Miles stared at her for a while, and something in her eyes seemed to satisfy him, for he nodded. "Now, I have called the three of you in here because there's an offer that I've been asked to make to the three of you."

"What offer is this?" Mary shifted uncomfortably on her seat. She was in her ninth month of pregnancy and according to the midwife who took care of her and Anne, they were due in about a week or so. Her greatest regret was that her baby would be born in prison and would probably never know freedom. The thought was heart breaking, but she was honest enough to admit that this sentence had really been fair. For one, they had comfortable beds to sleep in and enough food to eat. Even though they had to work hard, no one hit or shouted at them unnecessarily. Also, their welfare was important to their jailors. It was more than what they had done for Connie.

She bowed her head as she thought about their older sister who had turned out to be their maternal cousin. When she thought about the things that her parents had done to Connie, she wanted to weep and prostrate herself on behalf of her family and beg for forgiveness. She didn't even know if she would ever have the words to express her deep regrets at how Connie had been treated by her family.

The only thing that gave her a little bit of happiness in this place was that she never had to meet her parents. They were in another part of the house and much as she was learning to forgive them for getting her and her siblings into this mess, she still didn't trust them. For the two grownups to have ill-treated Connie by selling her to Mr. Pitcher and also her father trying to force himself on her was too much.

She and Anne had suffered at the hands of cruel men and lost their virtue to them. She now knew how Connie had felt when the man she had thought was her father had tried to destroy her virtue. It was a terrible feeling, and she just prayed that Connie would one day forgive them, all of them.

"Miss Baker," Mr. Miles was saying, and she looked up to find him and her siblings looking at her.

"I'm sorry."

"What I was putting to you is this. The three of you can choose to remain here for the rest of your lives and this means that your children will be born as prisoners too."

"What is the alternative," Mary asked.

"Freedom for the three of you but with certain conditions."

Once again, they gave him suspicious looks. "That sounds very strange indeed," Mary said.

"Well you can only decide how strange it is after you have listened to the offer." The siblings nodded. "Marriage for the two of you, and then your brother will go and live with one of you as long as you promise to watch over him carefully."

Anne took a deep breath. "Who is supposed to marry us and in our conditions?" She looked down at her swollen belly and shook her head slowly. "Who will bear this shame with us?"

"Have no fear about that, Miss Baker. There are two very good suitors who know everything they have to about you and still they offered for your hands in marriage. One of the conditions of the marriages is that they should happen immediately, should you agree, so that your children will be born within wedlock. This means that your children will grow up with fathers who will take care of them and also provide respectability for them. Otherwise your children will go about in life knowing they don't have fathers, and that is a very hard thing to bear. Why don't I give you a day or two to think about this and then you can give me your response then."

～

"Mary, I'm really scared," Anne whispered to her sister later that night when they were in the room they shared. "The offer we are being given sounded too good to be true, and it makes me afraid of what we might face should we agree."

"But what other choice do we have, Anne? Every day I see you and Grant locked up in this place, I die a little bit more. You're too young to have to suffer such, and I just wish you would be set free and they hold me here."

"The man talked about two gentlemen who are willing to take us as their wives so our children will have names and not be ostracized all their lives."

Mary nodded, "But what if the men turn out to be like our father and reject our children? Papa rejected Connie and he made her life a living hell."

"But that was because our mother allowed him to. We have learnt our lessons in this time that we've been here, and I, for one, will never let a man torment my child. I would rather die."

"It won't come to that, but I understand what you're feeling. According to me, the important thing is for us to be granted our freedom. Once we get married to the men, we shall know what kind of people they are. Definitely if they are kind and merciful, we can look forward to better lives than we've lived so far, Anne. However, if they turn out to be mean people, we can always find ways of getting out of their lives and the marriages. We are older and wiser now and can conduct ourselves with prudence."

"So, do you think we should accept the offer?"

"For Grant's sake, I will. Then I will take him with me and train him up to be a good man. See how John was so lucky because of his good heart. We used to reproach him for having a soft nature but in the end, he is the one who has benefitted. And I'll never forget what Abel once told us, that when we do good, we will reap good, but if we are evil then that's what we'll reap." She placed a hand over her big stomach. "This child may have been conceived in pain, shame and humiliation, but I refuse to be bitter toward him or her. May God help me to be a good mother and teach him or her the good values in life for in the end good will always triumph over evil."

"Thank you for saying that, Mary."

20
NEW BEGINNINGS

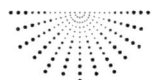

"Connie, may I please speak with you?" John entered the parlour where she was seated, and she nodded.

"What do you have on your mind?"

"I know that my parents and my siblings really did bad things to you, but I'm here to ask for your forgiveness on their behalf."

"John, I already forgave them and have nothing against them."

"I know that because you're a very kind person, Connie. But I also worry about them."

"You don't have to because they are now free. Your sisters and brother were granted a pardon just yesterday and they are now free." John paled. "Why do you look like you're not happy about the news."

"I'm happy that they are free but I'm also worried. What if they come here and try to harm you again?"

"They can never do that because the reports we received from the house keeper were that they have really done well and that is why they have been set free. They have changed and I want to believe that it is genuine and forever."

"So, will they come and live here with us?"

Connie shook her head. "It was thought best that they be found other good homes where they will live and thrive."

A relieved look came over John's face. "I didn't want them to suffer, but I also don't want them to ever hurt you again, Connie."

"Well since you'll soon find out anyway, Mary got married to Mr. Nathaniel Hunter who is the son of one of the wealthiest industrialists here in England. They will be making their home in Canada, and Grant is going with them. Anne also got married to Lord Elroy Fitzgerald, the son of a lowly baron, but he is a good man. Anne and her husband are being sent to Australia because he is an attaché to the mission out there. Well they won't leave immediately because they are due to put to bed any time now."

John observed her for a while, "You did this," it was more of a statement than a question. "Why when we were so mean to you?"

"Because I have learnt what forgiveness is, John. None of us is perfect in this world and we do a lot of wrong things. But there is grace if we are willing to change and walk on the right path."

"Thank you," he took her hand and placed it on his head. "I will serve you with my whole life."

Connie smiled at her brother, then something struck her, "You haven't asked about your parents."

"That's because they are in the place that is just right for us. With them out of all our lives, I believe that we can become good people eventually."

"I always say that you have wisdom beyond your years, John."

∼

"Some people look really happy," Abel walked into the living room where he found his wife and her brother grinning from ear to ear. "And something tells me that you have been reading something wonderful in the newspapers."

"See this," John pointed at the two notices that were side by side on the second page of the newspaper.

Abel bent down and smiled.

"In Paddington, the wife of Mr. Nathaniel Hunter, Mrs. Mary Hunter nee Baker, was delivered of a bouncing baby boy on the tenth of December the year of our Lord.

John Grant Hunter is the first grandchild of Industrialist Edward Hunter and his wife Doris, who are happy to announce that mother and child are alive and in a hopeful way."

"Congratulations are in order John and Connie on the birth of your nephew," Abel ruffled the young boy's hair. "How does it feel to be an uncle and have a nephew named after you?"

"It makes me feel old," John said with a cheeky grin on his face and they all laughed. "See, I'm an uncle twice." He pointed at the second notice.

"Born on the tenth of December the year of our Lord, to Lord Elroy and Lady Anne Fitzgerald nee Baker, a young cherub who has been named Constance Mary Fitzgerald. Little Lady Constance Mary is

the first grandchild of Lord Peter and Lady Amy Fitzgerald who are beyond themselves with joy.

A long and prosperous life is predicted for mother and child."

"Oh, and Connie you also have a child named for you," Abel felt pleased for his wife.

"It gives me so much joy," Connie hadn't met any of her sisters since they were released but seeing that Anne had named her child after her humbled her. She knew that it was her sister's way of apologizing for all the wrong things they had done to her and she had a feeling that had Mary also birthed a daughter, she would have done the same thing. She was sure the two girls had discussed the names for their children at length.

～

Connie knew that she was loved and the last six months since she had been married to Abel were the best times of her life. She had a large family even though she doubted that she would ever meet some of them. But she was hopeful that with time and after the wounds had healed, she and her sisters as well as Grant would come to a place where they could meet and be happy together.

Completely sure of her husband's love, she was now confident and very elegant. No one seeing her now could connect her to the young woman who had been crippled and tortured by her mother's sister and her husband.

"My joy is complete," Connie announced as she joined her husband in their bedchamber early that evening. He saw the sparkle in her eyes and his heart was at peace at last.

"Well, what's next? You have a nephew and a niece, and your sisters seem to have settled and been accepted in their new homes."

"Nothing," she kissed him on his lips and his hands went to her swollen stomach. "My sisters and brother are living comfortably now, and life is good. Asking for more is just being greedy, so all I can be is thankful for the mercies of the Lord."

"Do you think a time will come when you will visit Mary in Canada and Anne in Australia?"

Connie thought for a little while, "One can never tell what the future holds, and I won't dwell on that for now. That part of my life is over and much as I wish them well it's best for all of us if we remain as far apart from each other as possible, at least for now."

"And does John feel the same way? What if he decides that he wants to visit his siblings at some point?"

"That's a bridge that we'll cross when we get to it. But for now, he is content to be an uncle from a distance. That young man is mature beyond his years, and I'm thankful that we got the chance to bring him up. He'll be a good person one day."

"I have no doubt about that," Abel agreed. "And whatever you choose to do with regard to your family in the future, I'll be behind you all the way."

"My love, I'm just thankful that you and Captain Trent found good husbands for my sisters and they can have fresh new beginnings."

"We served with both men and knew them to be quite honourable. They have high regard for Captain Trent and when he suggested that they marry your sisters, they were only too happy to oblige him. You see, they owe him their lives and would do anything for him."

"I'm just happy that they are responsible men and will take good care of my sisters and their children."

With the sun setting outside, it's final rays throwing a golden glow over the landscape before darkness descended, Connie knew in the very depth of her being that morning does indeed come after even the longest of nights.

EPILOGUE

Connie drifted back from what seemed like a long journey and realised that she was lying in her own bed. She felt like she had come through a long battle and opened her eyes slowly. The room was flooded in light, and she squinted, wondering if it was day or night.

Then she heard the soft voice like a sniffle and looked around. Suddenly she saw her husband and Mrs. Lamb smiling at her. Her mother was standing beside the small bassinet with Mrs. Dawson and both of them were staring down in fascination.

"What is that noise," Connie croaked. Mrs. Lamb walked over to the bed as Connie's mother bent over the bassinet, then straightened up again. Then she walked toward the bed, smiling tenderly at Connie.

"It is our son," Abel sat at the head of the bed and pulled Connie into his arms. She winced but she also liked the feeling of her husband's strong arms around her. "My darling," he laughed, looking very happy. "The noise you are hearing is our very hungry son," he said, receiving the baby from Connie's mother and placing him in his Connie's arms. "You were so exhausted by childbirth that the doctor had to give you something to make you sleep so you could get enough rest. But this little one is so hungry and demanding for your attention."

Connie stared at the little pink face wrapped up in soft woollen clothes and felt the tears in her eyes. His hair was dark just like Abel's and something came alive deep within her.

He was so beautiful, the baby she and Abel had prayed and hoped for. This was their son; the fulfilment of their love.

With a joyous laugh like that of new mothers through the ages, she looked up at Abel.

"He is so beautiful," she told her husband, eyes brimming with happy tears. "My precious," she looked back down at the baby nestled in her arms. "Do open your eyes so I can see you."

And as if the baby understood her every word, he opened his eyes and she saw the deep green eyes, so beautiful and so intense, like Abel's.

"Oh!' She said with mock rage. "You have your father's hair, face and now the eyes too. What of mine, pray, do you have?"

Abel pulled them both close, snickering as he shared a happy look with the three older women. "I told you so, my dear Good Wife. The first three babies will all look like their very happy and doting Papa. You can lay claim to the next three who will be girls," he said, "And that's a promise."

"Oh, Abel Brian Pierson, you really did it this time."

"But isn't he beautiful," Abel reached out a hand and reverently touched his son's cheek. "And so hungry," as the baby's mouth moved as if searching for nourishment.

"Let me just nurse him and when he is satisfied, you can take him to his grandfathers since his grandmothers have already had some time with him," she said. Mrs. Lamb, Mrs. Dawson and Connie's mother nodded and walked out of the room, leaving the small family alone for the moment.

"This is our moment," Abel looked down at his wife as she nursed their baby. This beautiful woman who had gone through so much pain nearly her whole life, and yet she never became bitter or vengeful. She was so forgiving as well. "You are so beautiful, and I love you so much, Constance Pierson. And I'll spend the rest of my life making you happy so you will always be smiling."

Connie smiled as she looked up at her husband. "And I love you so much Abel Pierson."

She believed with her whole heart that he meant every word he'd said to her. And in their lifetime, her beloved husband fulfilled every good and wonderful promise he made to her.

∼

THANK YOU FOR CHOOSING A PUREREAD BOOK!

We hope you enjoyed the story, and as a way to thank you for choosing PureRead we'd like to send you this free book, and other fun reader rewards…

Click here for your free copy of Whitechapel Waif
PureRead.com/victorian

Thanks again for reading.
See you soon!

LOVE VICTORIAN ROMANCE?

If you enjoyed this story why not continue straight away with other books in our PureRead Victorian Romance library?

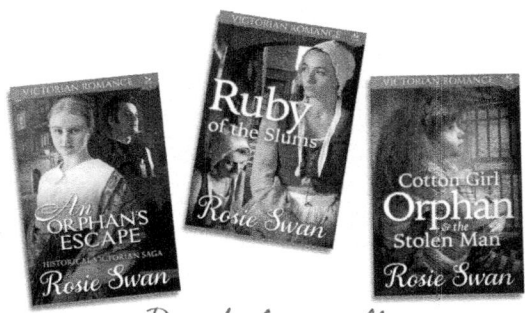

Read them all...

Orphan Christmas Miracle

An Orphan's Escape

The Lowly Maiden's Loyalty

Ruby of the Slums

The Dancing Orphan's Second Chance

Cotton Girl Orphan & The Stolen Man

Victorian Slum Girl's Dream

The Lost Orphan of Cheapside

Dora's Workhouse Child

Saltwick River Orphan

Workhouse Girl and The Veiled Lady

OUR GIFT TO YOU

AS A WAY TO SAY THANK YOU WE WOULD LOVE TO SEND YOU THIS BEAUTIFUL STORY FREE OF CHARGE.

Our Reader List is 100% FREE

Click here for your free copy of Whitechapel Waif

PureRead.com/victorian

At PureRead we publish books you can trust. Great tales without smut or swearing, but with all of the mystery and romance you expect from a great story.

Be the first to know when we release new books, take part in our fun competitions, and get surprise free books in your inbox by signing up to our Reader list.

As a thank you you'll receive an exclusive copy of Whitechapel Waif - a beautiful book available only to our subscribers...

Click here for your free copy of Whitechapel Waif

PureRead.com/victorian

Printed in Great Britain
by Amazon